I0822360

MY BILLIONAIRE PROFESSOR

A FORBIDDEN ROMANCE OF UNEXPECTED LOVE AND PASSION

MIMI WEST

CONTENTS

Prologue – Theo 5
1. Kaylee 9
2. Theo 17
3. Kaylee 27
4. Theo 37
5. Kaylee 47
6. Theo 57
7. Kaylee 67
8. Theo 77
9. Kaylee 87
10. Theo 97
11. Kaylee 107
12. Theo 115
13. Kaylee 125
14. Theo 135
15. Kaylee 145
16. Theo 155
17. Kaylee 165
18. Theo 175
19. Kaylee 185
20. Theo 195

References 207

PROLOGUE – THEO

Ring, ring.

I tear my eyes away from the pages of the book. I slide my bookmark into place before dropping the hardback onto my desk with a solid *thud*. I grab the phone from the receiver and place it next to my ear, holding it between my head and shoulder as I grab my glass of bourbon.

"Hello?" I take a sip.

"Theo? What's going on, old friend? It's Asher."

I swallow the warm liquid quickly as surprise washes over me. "Asher? It's good hearing from you—we haven't talked in months."

"I know. I've been so busy that I haven't had time for much else."

"That's right." I lean back in my desk chair, getting comfortable. "How's newly married life treating you?"

He chuckles. "Well, it isn't all that new anymore. We just celebrated our third wedding anniversary the other day."

"Wow, has it been that long already?" I roll my eyes, but my voice hides the fact that I'm not interested in his marriage in the slightest. Asher and I have been friends since we were kids. This is the kind of thing old friends talk about.

He laughs. "I know you don't give a shit. Don't act like you do," he laughs out loud.

I chuckle. "That's not entirely true," I reply. "I might not care how long you've been together, but I do care that you're still going strong and happy." I swirl the liquid in my glass. "You are happy, aren't you?"

"I am." And I can hear it in his voice.

"Good. That's all that matters then." I take a sip.

"I know I'm a shitty friend for not reaching out …"

"Not at all. That's life, Asher. Things come up; we have to dedicate our time to our careers and our families. Friends always come in last. There's no hard feelings."

"You didn't let me finish."

My brows lift.

"I don't want to be the friend who only calls when he needs something, but …" He sighs. "Well, I guess I don't really need anything, but I do have an opportunity for you."

I lean forward in my chair, my eyes moving over to watch the flames in the fireplace dance. "Oh, really?"

"The university I'm teaching at has had a job become available. We need someone to assist the students with getting the weekly paper out. Now, this job isn't for an editor position or anything like that. That's something one of the students does. It's more of a managing position. Do a little teaching—things they'll need in the real world. Go over articles and writing styles. That sort of thing."

"I've never run a newspaper in my life," I point out.

"No, but you do own and run several very popular magazines. How different can it be?"

I run my hand through my hair and chuckle. "I'm sure it's very different."

"Well, maybe so. But what do you have to lose? It's a guest position, so you'll only have to sign a contract for a year. Come to Chicago and get out of New York for a little while. Try your hand at teaching. Plus, who knows … You may find several good reporters that you want to hire in the future. It'll almost be like getting first pick of the freshies. Like my daughter. She's actually on the student paper."

He does have a point. I'm always on the lookout for some young, new writers. Writers are becoming few and far between as far as a full-time career goes. A career in writing can be very slow to start, and young people these days don't have the patience to stick with it. Plus, I like to get them young so they don't have time to pick up any bad habits.

"Ugh …" I mutter, leaning back and rubbing the back of my neck as I think it over.

"It's only a year of your life. And who knows … You might enjoy it. You always talk about looking for a change. This could be it. And if you end up not loving it, it's only for a year."

I nod. "Alright, let's do it."

KAYLEE

I walk into my apartment; the sound of a group of girls giggling hits my ears as I walk down the hallway and into the living room. "What's going on here?" I ask, looking at the four girls sitting around the room.

I drop my book bag onto the floor before kicking off my flip-flops.

"It's about time you got home. We've been waiting for you," Margo, my roommate, says. "Did you get all your books for the semester?"

I flop down onto the end of the couch, pulling a pillow into my lap. "Yep, all set."

"Good." She grins, twisting a strand of her auburn hair around her finger. "We were just discussing the plans for tonight."

I look from her to Julie, to Sarah, and then to Amber before bringing my eyes back to my roommate. "What plans?"

"Exactly. It's the last weekend before school starts back on Monday. We have to celebrate one last time."

I roll my eyes as my head falls back, resting against the couch. "How many times are you going to use this excuse?"

She frowns at me. "What do you mean? I didn't say last weekend was the last weekend before school starts."

I smile. "No, you said we only have a couple of weekends left before school starts. The weekend before that, you pointed out that we were quickly running out of weekends before school starts. And the weekend before that—"

"Yeah, yeah," she interrupts, waving her hand through the air to dismiss me. "You have barely gone out with us all summer." She trains her blue eyes on mine.

"Yeah, you haven't been much fun since you broke up with Travis," Julie says, the other girls nodding along in agreement.

Now, I can see this for what it truly is: them ganging up on me, trying to peer pressure me into going out. "I just don't want to bump into him anywhere," I breathe out.

"And we understand that," Margo says, taking my hand in hers. "But school is starting on Monday. You're going to be around him again, whether you like it or not. We may as well get one fun weekend before we're all stuck in class, doing homework, or at practice."

I bite on the inside of my cheek, thinking it over. Sure, they're kind of ganging up on me right now, but is that really a bad thing? I mean, I have friends who love me, who want me to go out with them for one last night of fun before school starts. And Margo is right about Travis. I'll have to be around him again, whether I like it or not. He's on the football team, and I'm on the cheer squad. We run in the same circle. There's no avoiding him once we're thrown back into school life.

I roll my eyes. "Well, I'm supposed to have dinner with my dad and stepmom tonight, but I guess if I can get out of that …"

They all cheer and bounce around with excitement.

Margo practically pushes me off the couch. "Go, call him, and cancel."

Clutching my phone in my hand, I move into my bedroom. I scroll through my contact list until I find his name, then I push call and move the phone to my ear. It rings a few times before he picks up.

"Hey, hun. What's up?"

I wrinkle my nose and clench my eyes shut, preparing myself to say the words I know he'll hate. "Hey Dad, I'm really sorry, but I'm going to have to get a raincheck on dinner tonight."

"What? Why?"

I roll my eyes as I turn and walk the other way. "I just have a lot going on right now with school starting up on Monday. I'm like a chicken with its head cut off, trying to get everything ready. I'm exhausted after spending the week with Mom. Then, I spent the day running around and getting books and supplies. I just walked in, and I'm so tired I can barely move. I think I'm just going to order some dinner, unpack from my trip home, get a long shower, and go to bed early because tomorrow is another busy day."

He takes a deep breath, letting it out slowly. "This dinner is special, Kay. Remember, I told you that my friend is joining us? It's important that you meet him and put in a good word for yourself. He's taking over the management position at the paper. You get in good with him, and it could be the start of a long writing career after graduation."

"Yeah, I know, Dad, but can't you just put in that good word for me? I mean, I know you already have every single article I've written for that paper tucked away in a scrapbook. Show him the book, talk me up, and tell him I'm sorry I couldn't be there to meet him in person. After school starts and the new wears off, after things settle down, we can reschedule."

"But he'll already know you by that point," he points out.

I lace my fingers into my hair, pushing it back. "I know, Dad, but it's the best I can do right now. Please understand. You remember what it was like your senior year, right? I'll barely have time to take a breath once school starts. I need tonight, self-care, mental-break kind of night."

He sighs. "Alright," he reluctantly agrees.

"Thank you. I'll see you Monday on campus." I hang up before he can say anything else.

I drop my phone onto the mattress as I fall back, staring up at the ceiling.

I should probably feel bad for canceling on my dad, but the truth is that I don't. Actually, I'm kind of relieved that I don't have to deal with him tonight. I've been dreading this dinner all week.

I'm sure I sound like a horrible daughter, but the two of us just aren't all that close. He and my mom met and fell in love when they were still in high school. My mom became pregnant with me in her senior year, and she gave birth to me soon after graduation. Because she was a young mother, she didn't get to go to college like most kids her age. My dad, however, did go to college. He told my mom that he was going so he could get a good job that would provide for us all.

He was a full-time student, and he worked to make money for us whenever he wasn't in school. My mom, she stayed home and took care of me. To supplement their income, she babysat all the local kids in the neighborhood. Eventually, though, the two drifted apart, and they split. Dad moved out, leaving me with my mom. We never did the court-appointed visitation thing. He tried for a while, but I always threw a fit as a kid, and eventually, he gave up. Instead of spending every other weekend and holiday with him, he'd stop by on my birthday and Christmas, give me a gift, and leave.

It wasn't until I hit my teenage years that the two of us started to click. I was old enough to understand what happened with him and my mom, and I no longer blamed him. I understood that people grow and change, and he and my mom just grew at different paces. It wasn't anyone's fault, exactly. I was also old enough to understand that he did try when it came to me. I was the one to put an end to our relationship. Once I realized that, our relationship slowly got better and stronger. But then he got married.

I didn't care that he was getting married. It's not like I expected him and my mom to get back together, but once he got married, it became clear that she was his top priority. Not me. The calls slowed, and he no longer came over on Christmas. Instead, he wanted me to go to him because she wanted a traditional Christmas. And I did go a few times.

Meredith and I, we just don't click. I'm a realist, while she ... Well, she likes to pretend that everything is better than it is. She has to have everything around her reflect their perfect life: their big house, her fancy car, their perfect marriage. No matter how hard she tried, I never fit into their perfect little picture because I'm proof that my dad isn't perfect. He had a life before her. But what does she expect? He's a good ten years older than her. Of course, he had a life before she came along. The worst part is that she's also a professor at school, so it's almost impossible to avoid them.

A knock on my bedroom door pulls me from my thoughts.

Margo pops her head into my room. "Well?"

I give her a smile. "Schedule is clear."

"Yes!" she breathes out, her hand turning to a fist as she jerks her arm in a downward motion. She then points her index finger at me. "Get dressed and look hot. We're leaving at eight." Without another word, she pulls my door shut and rushes away. I laugh when I hear her excitedly telling the others the news.

Pushing myself up, I move to my closet to find the perfect outfit. Margo is right. School is about to start, and I need to get myself back into the swing of things. I'm young, and you only live once. There's no sense in wasting the best years of my life just to avoid seeing the guy who I broke up with months ago. Surely, he's moved on by now anyway.

I strip and pull on a black minidress. It's short, ending mid-thigh. It's tight, hugging every curve, and it has thin spaghetti straps, so my arms, neck, and upper chest are all exposed. I pull on a pair of socks and my favorite military boots; then, I take a black and red flannel from my closet. I slide my arms into it and tie it up at my waist, knowing it will be off and tied around my waist by the end of the night.

My long black hair hangs to my lower back. I turn in the mirror and make sure it's still straight and smooth. I pull a brush through it to take out any tangles, and then I focus on my makeup. I add dark liner, long lashes, and a dark red lip. I contour, bronze, and highlight. Giving myself a once over, I approve of the look and slip out of my room, ready to get this night started.

"Look at you!" Margo gushes, walking a circle around me when I step into the living room. "Damn, girl. I thought you forgot how to look hot. Good to see you got your groove back."

I roll my eyes. "I never lost it. I just took a break." I shrug, one hand on my hip.

She laughs and hooks her arm with mine. "Let's go. We're meeting the others at the club. How much do you want to bet that Julie will be late?"

We both laugh as we make our way out to the street.

THEO

"Do you need anything else before I leave for the night, sir?"

"No, Jefferson. Thank you."

He nods. "Don't forget the bottle of wine that is on the entryway table for you to grab as you walk out. If you need anything, just give me a call."

"Thank you, Jefferson," I reply, not looking away from my computer screen.

I officially made the move from New York to Chicago less than a week ago. I'm glad that Jefferson came with me. I have no idea what I'd do if he didn't. Jefferson has been the highest-paid staff member I've had for the last ten years, and with good reason. He does a little of everything, and he does anything I ask. He prepares my meals or orders out at my request. He keeps the place clean; he drives me places if I need him to. He keeps the house stocked up with food and supplies, and he keeps me on schedule. This week, he's been the one to unpack and get the new apartment in order while I've stayed buried in work here in my home office.

I was looking forward to this move, and I wanted a break from the magazines, but now I see how much harder this is going to be. Instead of being at the office, I'm taking phone call after phone call and doing all my meetings online. I tell myself that things will slow down once everyone is used to me being gone. Until then, I just have to be patient while we all work to adjust to this change.

I push away from my desk and head down the hallway to my bedroom. I pull my shirt over my head as I pass through into the bathroom to take a shower. I've had this dinner planned with Asher since I agreed to take the position. I've been in town for a week now, but I've been swamped with work and trying to get settled. I'm not sure if this dinner is to welcome me to town, if it's just two friends catching up, or if he's trying to get his daughter some bonus points since she's one of the students I'll be dealing with at the paper. Either way, I can't put it off any longer.

I take a shower, shave, and get dressed. It's just a casual dinner at his home, so I dress in jeans and a button-down shirt. I grab my wallet, phone, keys, and the bottle of wine from the entryway table before walking out the door. My Uber is waiting by the curb, so I climb into the backseat, putting my wireless earbuds into my ears to avoid conversation on the drive over. He doesn't live too far out of the city, but with traffic, it takes us almost an hour to get there. I climb out of the car, leaving a tip on my phone as I make my way up the sidewalk.

I slide my phone into my pocket as I look up at the house. I smile because this is the kind of home I imagined he'd end up living in. It's a big, white Colonial with large windows and black shutters. The front of the porch is lined with shrubs, and a row of flowering plants runs the length of the sidewalk on either side, right to the gate of the white picket fence. The front porch is decorated like something out of a fall issue of Home and Gardens. I know we're starting the fall semester at school, but it's still very much summer weather.

There's a porch swing on one end. On the other is a couple of rocking chairs with a table between them. On the table is a black lantern. There are black and white checkered pillows and a welcome rug in front of the door. I push the doorbell as I turn to give it all one more look, noticing the red and yellow Mums on the steps.

The door opens, and I spin back around, finding Asher with a big smile.

He holds out his hand to shake. "How ya doing, old friend?"

I slap my hand into his, and he pulls me in for a hug. "It's good seeing you."

He pats my back. "Come on in. You have to meet Meredith."

I follow him in, finding the house to be exactly what I expected it to be. There's a large staircase in the foyer and a beautiful living room with a big fireplace to the right, but he leads me to the left. Pushing his way through the swinging door, I find us walking into the large kitchen. It's the perfect family home—one you'd see a large family of your favorite TV sitcom live in—the kind that makes you wonder how exactly they manage to afford it. The woman, whom I'm assuming is Meredith, looks up from her place behind the stove.

Her brows lift, and her blue eyes show surprise when she looks at me. "Oh, I didn't realize our guest was here already." She dries her hands as she makes her way around the island. "It's nice to finally meet you. Asher has told me so much about you over the years."

I shake her hand and hold up the bottle of wine. "A little thank you for the invitation."

"How nice of you. I'll just get this chilling." She takes the bottle from my hands. "Asher, do you want to offer our guest a drink in your study since dinner isn't quite done?" She sweeps her blonde hair behind her ear.

"Of course," he agrees. "I just got a brand new bottle of scotch I've been needing an excuse to open." He pats me on the back, leading me out of the kitchen. He takes me down the hall before entering what looks like a home office. There's a small bar in the corner, and he steps up behind it. "So, tell me: how are you liking Chicago?"

I step up to the bar and nod. "I haven't seen much of it yet. The office is having a hard time without me, so it seems I've spent more time working with New York than I spent working when I was in New York."

He smiles and nods as he pours our drinks. "I'm sure they'll get used to your absence eventually."

I take the glass he offers, holding it up. He taps his glass off mine, and we both take a sip.

"Unfortunately, my daughter will not be able to make it to dinner tonight." I can hear the bitterness in his words.

"Oh? Why not?" I swirl the liquid in my glass.

"Oh, you know how it is your senior year. Did you have time for your father?"

I scoff. "No way."

He nods. "Exactly." He sighs and shakes his head. "She says she's just too busy, that she's been running around trying to get everything together for school to start on Monday. She's a good student, so I find it hard to believe that she hasn't done that already. She's not usually the kind that waits until the last minute."

I smirk. "She probably just has something better to do," I joke.

He laughs. "I'm sure she does." He shrugs. "I expect her to stand me up, but I'm sorry she did it on a night you were expecting to meet her."

I wave my hand through the air. "You said she's on the paper, right? I'm sure I'll meet her on Monday."

Meredith pops her head into the room. "Dinner is served." She beams a wide smile.

"We'll be right there, hun," Asher tells her, motioning toward his glass that still has a little left in it.

She nods, her long blonde curls bouncing. "Take your time."

When she walks away, I throw back the rest of my drink, and Asher does the same.

"I'm really glad you took this position," he says, leading the way to the dining room. "I know when it comes to successful writing careers, you're the person that Kay needs to be learning from."

"Oh, well … I don't write anymore," I point out.

He walks into the dining room and takes his seat. "No, but that's because you don't have to. You worked your way up, made yourself a real success story. I mean, how many people can say they came from an upper-middle-class home and turned themselves into a self-made billionaire?"

Meredith's brows raise, and her blue eyes slide over to me. "What is it that you do again?"

Asher chuckles. "Honey, I told you. He started Suits Magazine, the magazine for men."

She nods. "Oh, that's right. You did tell me that." She looks over at me. "And didn't you start a new one a few years back for women?"

I nod. "I did."

"Heels," she said, snapping her fingers. "You know, we actually have this month's copy of both. I should get you to sign them while you're here." She beams a wide smile as she picks up her wine glass.

I want to laugh, but I hold it back. "Sure, I'd love to." It's been a while since I signed one of the magazines my company produces. In fact, I don't think I've signed one since the very first one. It's now framed and hanging in the lobby of the building in New York.

"Don't bother him with stuff like that," Asher tells his wife as he picks up his fork and knife.

She shrugs as her eyes narrow on him like he's chastising her. "He said he didn't mind doing it. It's not like I meet a billionaire every day."

I lean forward, holding up my hands. "Please, I'm just like any other person. Nothing special."

Asher is already digging into his dinner, and Meredith is moving her food around her plate. She looks to be more interested in the wine than anything else.

Her blue eyes meet mine once again. "I'm sorry, but I have to know: Why is a billionaire who could be anywhere in the world dedicating a year of his life to handle some students at a college newspaper here in Chicago?"

I pick up my glass of wine and take a sip. "It's not something I expect anyone to understand, really. People think that having money will fix everything. The truth is that money usually complicates everything. Sure, I could be lying on a beach in the Caribbean right now, but I've done that time and time again. Life doesn't hold much value when you have nothing to do." I shrug. "Why not pass along the knowledge I have while I can?"

She takes a small bite of her roasted potato. "Are you saying that working gives your life purpose, and without it, you feel ... useless?"

I sit a little straighter. "I don't know about useless, but I definitely feel lost when I spend too much time away from work. I try to keep a balance to everything I do. I work, but I also take vacations. This job is me trying something new. And who knows? Maybe I'll find a few students who I can take under my wing. I'm sure if they're looking for a career in writing, they'll jump at the chance of working for me in New York."

Meredith's eyes stretch wide as acknowledgment washes over her. "Oh, did you tell him about Kay?" she asks Asher.

He wipes his mouth with his cloth napkin. "Of course I did. That's why she was supposed to join us for dinner tonight. So they could meet ahead of time."

Meredith looks back at me. "She's an amazing writer. I think we have every article she's written for the paper. We can dig them out for you after dinner if you'd like."

I hold up my hand. "Thank you, but I think I'd prefer to wait. I'll be meeting her on Monday, and I don't want any presumed ideas about her or her writing." I pick up my glass of wine. "So, why don't we just enjoy this dinner, catch up like old friends?" I say, looking at Asher. Then I turn and look at his wife. "Get to know one another like new friends, and forget about next week and the reason I'm really here. Huh?"

"Agreed." Asher picks up his glass of wine, and he holds it in the air.

I do the same, and then we both look at Meredith until she follows. We all take a sip of our wine and finally get to eating the delicious-looking steak, roasted potatoes, steamed vegetables, and warm dinner rolls.

It's been a long time since I've had a casual dinner with friends. Usually, I have dinner alone, with a date, and sometimes over a business meeting. There's always an agenda, but tonight, we're free to just enjoy a meal and talk like the old friends we are, and I learn that I miss this side of things. Asher and I haven't been close in years, but it's nice getting to know this older, more mature version of him, and it's great getting to see him happy with Meredith. After dinner, we retire to the living room, where we have an after-dinner drink. I sign those magazines for Meredith, and I order a ride home. When my car arrives, they show me to the door, standing there smiling and waving until my car pulls away from the curb.

I take a deep breath, letting it out slowly as I roll the sleeves of my shirt up my forearms. I had a lovely time, but it's also nice getting away because now I don't have to pretend like I'm interested in conversations I have no interest in. I no longer have to force smiles or laughs to be polite.

I watch out the window as we make the drive back into the city. The darkness changes to bright lights, and the grass and trees turn into concrete sidewalks and brick buildings. Even though I intended on going straight home, I find myself telling the driver to pull over on a busy city street. I climb out, leave a nice tip for the driver, and make my way toward the doors of a very busy nightclub. May as well have one last drink before calling it a night. And who knows … maybe I'll meet someone to have a drink with?

KAYLEE

"To us and the best senior year we could ask for," Margo says, holding her shot in the air.

We all grab a glass. We tap them together, and then everyone throws back the clear liquid. My face wrinkles when the taste of the tequila finally sets in. I swallow it down quickly and pick up the slice of lime. I bite down, sucking the sour juice and swallowing it down to help rid my mouth of the burn. Tossing the lime down, I quickly chase the shot with a large gulp of beer.

"Whooooo!" a couple of the girls cheer as they throw their arms in the air.

"Come on. Let's hit the dance floor," Julie tells Sarah. She grabs her wrist and pulls her to the floor. They're quickly eaten up by the crowd.

Amber is already in the bathroom, probably crying and fighting with her on-again/off-again boyfriend, leaving just Margo and me at the table.

She leans back, crossing her legs, as her fingers mindlessly comb through her auburn hair.

"You see why I wasn't exactly excited about coming out?"

She frowns. "Why?"

"Amber is in the bathroom, probably crying, and we haven't even been here ten minutes. Those two are already on the hunt for a couple of guys to buy their drinks for the night."

She smiles and shrugs.

"It's only a matter of time before you go off with some guy, leaving me alone." I roll my eyes.

She leans forward so I can hear her over the music. "Then why don't you find a guy to entertain you for the night?"

I scoff. "I thought this was girls' night? Why does girls' night always end up with guys?"

She laughs and shrugs. "They make it more fun. You used to agree, remember?"

She's talking about our freshman year when we'd go out and end the night leaving separately. The only thing is, I would leave with Travis. The two of us started dating, and everything was fine until the breakup. Now, I'm not really sure how to do this whole single thing again.

"You're going to have to get back on the horse eventually, Kay."

I bite my lower lip as my eyes sweep over the crowded bar. "I know. I'm just not sure how." My eyes settle on a man who's making his way up the stairs to the VIP section. I don't know why, but I follow his every step. He has dark hair and even darker eyes. He's wearing a fitted white button-up shirt, the sleeves rolled up to his elbows. It's stretching across his broad chest and shoulders, and it's tucked into his black dress pants, showing off his narrow waist. His clothing fits him to perfection, giving everyone the perfect idea of what's beneath. The bouncer at the top of the stairs removes the rope and lets him through. When he does that, he's no longer in my line of sight, and my eyes move back to Margo.

She's looking at me with her brows raised, like she's waiting on my reply.

"Sorry, what?" I shake my head clear.

She grins. "Something cute just walk by?"

I roll my eyes. "Shut up. Let's just try having fun, huh?"

She grabs another shot from the tray in the center of the table. "Now you're talking." She holds it up.

Rolling my eyes, I grab another, tap it against hers, and then throw it back. I chase it down just like I did before, only now my blood is starting to warm from the alcohol pumping through my veins.

"Time to dance?"

"Let's do it," I agree.

She grabs my wrist and pulls me out onto the dance floor next to Julie and Sarah. To my surprise, Amber even makes her way out of the bathroom to join us. We dance together in one big group, swaying to the beat of the music and spinning around in a fit of giggles. Somehow, I feel every muscle start to relax as the stress starts to melt away.

My blood gets hotter and hotter, and I remove my flannel shirt and tie it around my waist. The cool air in the club feels good to my overheated skin that's slightly glistening with sweat. I move the cup in my hand to my lips, tilting my head back to swallow a gulp. With my head tipped back, my eyes open, and they land on the same man as earlier. He's leaning against the balcony of the VIP section overhead, his dark eyes trained on me.

I feel my skin break out in goosebumps, and the butterflies in my stomach come alive, fluttering their wings with excitement. I let my cup fall from my lips, and I smile up at him. He doesn't return my smile, but his eyes narrow slightly when he sees mine. Margo bumps my shoulder, getting my attention.

"Yes! Go after him. He's hot as hell." She fans her face with her hand as she continues to dance to the beat of the music. It's only now that I realize that I've stopped dancing.

My eyes move back up to him, finding him still watching, and it makes my blood burn hotter. The alcohol I've been consuming is starting to take effect, and I find myself wanting to draw this guy in. I turn my back to him and start to sway my hips back and forth. Margo grins at me, knowing the game I'm playing because it's one I've helped her play many times over the years. She starts to dance with me, her hand landing on my hip as we move together.

"He's watching you," she whispers. "Move your hips more."

I roll my eyes and laugh. "I'm going for another drink. You'll have to hold the floor down without me." I walk away, moving up to the bar, where I order another beer. Margo likes to pull guys in with her sex appeal. I, on the other hand, have more luck playing hard to get. While I'm in line at the bar, I refuse to look over my shoulder. I get my beer, and then I move over to our table. I have a seat, cross my legs, and take a sip. I don't look up for him until my head is tipped back, but he's still there, watching, just like I knew he would be.

I set my glass on the table, and I smile up at him. This time, he shoots back a smirk. He drags his eyes from mine as he turns his head to the side, looking in another direction. Maybe it's my imagination. Maybe he hasn't been checking me out. Maybe he's just meeting my gaze.

Margo sits at the table next to me with a fresh drink of her own. She leans in. "So … Are you going to go up there?"

I shrug. "I don't know. What if he's not interested in me?"

She snorts and rolls her eyes. "Girl, did you see the way he was looking at you?"

I can't help but smile. "Have you ever seen him here before? Does he look familiar at all?"

She's taking a sip of her drink, but she shakes her head. "I haven't seen him before. Maybe he's new to town or just passing through. Either way, you need to finish getting your groove back before school starts on Monday."

I snort. "Why in the world do I need to get laid before school starts?"

Her brows lift in shock. "Duh, several reasons."

I motion with my finger for her to list them off.

She sighs. "First of all, everyone knows that you're more relaxed after getting laid. And you seriously need to relax. Plus, you haven't been serviced in a very long time—"

"Serviced?" I laugh, shaking my head.

"If you get your needs met tonight, you'll be able to give your schoolwork your full attention. You won't have to worry about being in cheer practice and watching the boys tackle each other while thinking about how your ovaries are going to explode."

I laugh harder now, picking up my drink.

"And the final reason I can come up with in a split second is that Travis will take one look at you and know you haven't been with anyone since him."

I don't know if that's true, but I say, "So?"

"So?" Her eyes narrow on me. "He's been with at least four different girls this summer that I know of. You don't want him winning this breakup."

It doesn't bother me to hear about how many girls Travis has replaced me with. Actually, I'm happy that he's moving on and kind of impressed that he managed to land so many in three months. "There is no winner and loser in a breakup," I explain. "A breakup is just a breakup. In fact, one could say that the person who did the breaking up is the winner, while the person that was broken up with is the loser." I point my finger at her, proud of myself for one-upping her.

She laughs. "Oh, Kay … How do you know so little? A breakup is a game. Okay? Are you following?"

I feel stupid for even listening, but I nod.

"The person who does the breaking up scores the first point. But the breakup isn't the end. It's the beginning. You can score points for all sorts of things. And right now, Travis has at least four points, while you still only have the one."

I massage my temples because she's giving me a headache. "Okay, if what you're saying is true, when does this game end? How many points until it is the end?"

She shrugs. "There is no limit. And it ends when one of the parties gets invested in another relationship. So …" She grins and leans forward, her eyes moving back up to the balcony. "Go after that one. He's hot as hell, and he'll score you at least four points. Plus, something tells me you'll have plenty of fun letting him service you."

"You're impossible. You know that?" I arch my brow at her, but a grin pulls at my lips anyway.

She shrugs, leaning back in her seat.

My eyes move back up to the balcony, and to my surprise, he's still there, watching me. When our eyes meet, he clenches his teeth, making his jaw flex. His Adam's apple bobs in his throat, and he wets his lips.

I lean back in my chair and cross my legs as I bring my glass to my lips, thinking it over. I can't ignore the way my body is responding to him. And maybe Margo is right—not about the whole winning the breakup stuff, but about the need to relax before school starts. It has been a very long time since

I've been to bed with anyone. Travis and I have been broken up for three months now, and I've yet to move on. Plus, the last few months of our relationship were a bit rocky, and we weren't spending as much time in bed as we used to. Margo may be full of shit, but she's right about one thing: I need to get laid. Even thinking about it has the junction between my legs throbbing. I flex my thighs, and the pressure there helps to dull the need.

She glances up at him before bringing her eyes back to mine. "He's older. More experienced. I bet he'll be the best you've ever had."

I laugh and shake my head. "I've never been with an older man before. Have you?"

She nods. "Last year, when I was doing that internship, remember?"

I nod and smile. "That's right. You slept with your boss on the last day of the job."

She grins and nods. "Seriously, best sex ever."

I feel my face heat up from talking so openly about this, but I'm dying to know, so I lean in. "What's the biggest difference between a guy our age and an older man?"

She grins, wets her lips, and then bites down on her lower lip as she thinks it over. "I'm not saying that one is better than the other. They're just different. And it's a nice change-up when you've only ever been with younger guys. Older guys ..." She sighs. "They just know how to do it. They know how to sweep you off your feet because they've been doing it for years. It's like they got the whole thing down to an exact science. They know what to say to pull you in. They know how to touch you, how to tease you without it seeming like they're coming on too strong. They know that part of the fun is working up to *it*. And then, when you actually get to *it* … they take pride in making you feel good. It's like, the more they make you come undone, the more it says about them."

I take a deep breath to cool off my overheated body. "So young guys go hard and fast, and older guys take their time, tease, and build you up?"

"Yes and no." Her eyes move up, and she smiles. "Older guys are the best of both worlds. They can take their time, tease, and build you up just to watch you fall. Or …" She shrugs, eyes moving back to mine. "They'll bend you over their desk and fuck you until you scream." She smiles and nods. "They're extremely talented at doing both."

I laugh and finish off my drink. "I take it your old boss bent you over his desk."

Her cheeks are slightly pink, and her eyes are glazed over as she smiles and nods. "Oh yeah. He didn't let up until I was—"

"Alright." I hold my hand up. "I love you, but some things I don't need to know. I'm going for another drink." Without another word, I stand and walk to the bar with my empty glass. I find a couple of empty barstools at the far end, so I take one as I set my empty glass in front of me, waiting until I can get a bartender's attention.

I'm looking toward my table when I feel someone slide into the barstool to my left. Then my blood warms, goosebumps prickle my skin, and every hair stands on end. My heart starts to race, and I'm not sure why. That is, until I look to my left and find myself face-to-face with the man who's been watching me from the VIP balcony.

My back goes ramrod straight, and my mouth falls open, even though no words come out.

His dark blue eyes move around my body before settling on my face. He offers me a smirk and holds out his hand to shake. "I'm Theo. Is this seat taken?"

THEO

The woman I've been watching slides her hand into mine, and the moment we touch one another, I feel a wave of tingles racing up my arm. Her green eyes are sparkling, almond shaped, and lined in dark liner and long black lashes. She has a thin face with high cheekbones and a strong jaw. Her lips, they're painted dark red, but they're plump and glossy. The longer I look at them, the more I imagine how sweet they'd taste.

"Kay." Her voice is soft and delicate.

I can't help the smile that tugs at my lips as I hold her hand in mine. "It's nice to meet you. Can I buy you a drink?"

She gives me a lopsided grin, and her green eyes move to her empty glass before meeting mine. She nods. "Sure."

I wave my hand for the bartender, and he stops in front of us immediately.

She leans forward. "Two beers and two shots of tequila with lime."

He nods and rushes off to fill her order.

I turn back to her. "I was up in VIP, and I noticed you dancing with your friends. Is it a girls' night out?"

She puts her elbow on the bar, and she turns in her stool, the toe of her shoe grazing against my shin, and it makes my body tingle. "I guess you could say that."

I wet my lips. "So … I don't need to worry about some guy walking up behind me and hitting me over the head before carrying you away?"

She bites her lower lip and shakes her head slightly. "I'm on my own, if that's what you're asking."

I nod. "It is."

"And you?"

My eyes find hers. "I'm single."

Her smile widens. "Good. Now that that's settled, why don't we have a little fun?" She reaches for the shot the bartender just set down.

I toss some money to pay for the drinks, and then I pick up the little plastic shot glass of clear liquid. There's a lime on top, but she takes it off, motioning for me to take the shot.

I throw it back quickly. When I set the shot glass down, she's holding up the slice of lime between us. I lean in, biting the slice and sucking the juice. She discards the lime into my empty glass before picking up her shot.

I remove the lime slice from the top and watch as she pours the liquid into her mouth. She swallows, and a fire lights in her irises as I hold up the slice of lime between us. She leans in, biting the lime while keeping her eyes locked with mine. I don't know why, but watching her bite the lime I'm holding between my fingers only makes me imagine something else of mine dangerously close to those lips.

She pulls back, leaving the peel of the lime wedge in my hand as she picks up her beer. She takes a sip and then looks me up and down. "Come on." She slides off the barstool. "Let's dance." She grabs my hand and pulls me to the dance floor.

I take my beer with me, taking a large gulp as she finds our spot on the floor. Finally, she spins around, wrapping her arms around my neck. She pulls herself closer before starting to wiggle against me to the beat of the music. There's something about her eyes that is so familiar, but I can't put my finger on it. They're a beautiful shade of green—darker on the outer edge and vibrant and light around the pupil. They're slightly glassy, probably from drinking, but it makes them sparkle and light up under the multicolored lights of the club.

I'm no stranger when it comes to beautiful women. When you're a billionaire who lives in New York, who's as well-known as I am because of the work I do, women practically throw themselves at you. I've dated actresses, musicians, models, and socialites—all of them gorgeous, famous, and/or filthy fucking rich.

Whoever this woman is in front of me, she's got something none of them had. She has an edge. She isn't like the other women in here tonight. Her face isn't heavily caked in makeup. She doesn't have overly fake-looking lashes or those long plastic nails. She's not dripping in diamonds and gold or dressed head to toe in pink. She's naturally beautiful, going against social norms. She's wearing military boots with a tight-fitted dress. She has a black and red flannel around her waist, and her long, black hair is straight and sleek instead of highlighted and blonde.

She gets more than her fair share of attention. Her different style draws them in, but her beauty traps them, and I'm no different. She pulled me in like a bee to honey, and I'm more than happy with giving her whatever she wants: a dance, an evening, a night … she can have it all as long as she keeps looking at me with those hypnotic green eyes of hers.

"You new around here?" She spins around, pressing her back against my chest.

My hand squeezes her hip while I enjoy the feeling of her rounded ass rubbing against my groin. I dip my head forward, running the tip of my nose up her neck to her ear. "Just moved here a week ago," I say quietly.

She lifts her arm above her head, placing her hand on the back of my neck. She laces her fingers into my hair, her naturally long nails scratching my scalp and sending shivers down my spine. "How you like it?" She spins back around, her chest pressing against mine.

"I like it a little better now."

She grins and pulls her eyes away.

I take a drink of my beer as we continue to dance against one another. "Your friends aren't going to be mad that I've stolen you away, are they?"

She glances toward them, and when she does so, their eyes dash away, knowing they've been caught. She laughs and shakes her head. "They won't be mad. I think they're hoping this would happen. They say I haven't been any fun since my breakup."

"Who in their right mind would be dumb enough to break up with a beautiful woman like you?"

She rolls her eyes. "I broke up with him."

"Then why haven't you been any fun?"

She shrugs. "I wasn't trying to rub his nose in anything. I just kind of …" She takes a deep breath and wets her lips. "I took a step back, blended into the shadows."

"Something tells me you've never blended in in your life."

Her cheeks burn a little hotter. "A girl can try." She resists the smile that's tugging at her lips, instead, running her tongue across and wetting them.

"You ever been up in the VIP section?"

Her green eyes move up to the balcony as she shakes her head.

"You want to check it out? It's a little more private up there."

Her brows arch as her eyes move back to mine. "Private? What do we need privacy for?"

I shrug as my hand falls from her hip. "So we can get to know one another a little better." I lift my empty hand, brushing a strand of her raven-colored hair away from her cheek. "What do you say?"

She bites her lower lip before nodding. "Okay, sure."

I catch her hand in mine as I lead the way toward the staircase. At the top, the bouncer unfastens the red, velvet rope, letting us through. I take her to the back, past the small dance floor in the center, past the bar, past the tables and booths. In the very back section of the VIP area are sofas and sectionals. Each seating area is broken up by half walls, while the top half is tented glass. I have a seat at one end of the sofa, and she sits directly next to me, in the center—I take this as a good sign. She's sitting next to me instead of on the opposite end.

I take a drink of my beer before setting it on the coffee table before us. I lean back, stretching my right arm across the back of the couch. "Why don't you tell me a little about yourself."

She rolls her eyes as she leans forward to set down her beer. "Why don't we skip that part?" Her eyes are back on mine.

"Alright. Then what do you want to talk about?"

She wets her lips. "Nothing. I think there's a better way to use our time. Don't you?"

Ever so slowly, her hand comes to rest on my chest while she leans in to kiss me. I can feel how nervous she is, though. I see the doubt and worry in her eyes, and as badly as I want this moment between us, I can't help but wonder why she's moving so fast if she isn't entirely sure. Then I realize that it probably has something to do with the breakup she mentioned. She hasn't had her rebound yet, and now, she's just racing through to try and get it over with.

I'm torn between pulling back and pushing forward. I don't know how old this woman is, but I can tell she's young—even though she's old enough to be in here drinking due to the OVER 21 stamp on the back of her hand. I don't want to be a mistake for her. But at the same time, it seems pretty clear that she came out tonight with the intention of hooking up with someone. If I turn her down now, she could very well get offended and walk away from me, find a guy who won't treat her as well as I will. So, really, would pulling away from her do her any favors? I think not.

My hand cups her jaw, and I lean forward all in one smooth motion. My lips capture hers, and she gasps against them. I feel the cool air rush past my lips as she sucks it into her lungs. With her lips now parted, my tongue edges forward, slowly, teasingly testing the waters. I just barely taste her lips, and when she doesn't pull away, I push further. My tongue slides into her mouth, finding hers. The two twist and dance, tease and taste.

Her hand was splayed across my chest; now it's turning into a fist as she pulls me closer by my shirt. I keep one hand on her jaw, holding her to me. The other falls down to her thigh. Her skin is soft and warm, smooth. I run it up higher to her hip, squeezing to keep myself grounded. Right now, all I want to do is slide between her legs as I lay her back against this couch, covering her body with mine. But we're in public, and I can't do that. Still, I don't know if she's comfortable enough yet to go home with me. I know this is the age of hooking up, but this is Chicago, and bad things happen to women who are too trusting nowadays.

My body comes alive, and it becomes apparent when her hand falls from my chest. It falls into my lap and, innocently enough, brushes against the hardness in my pants. She moves it away, but I know she felt it, so I slow the kiss and break it off completely. My hand is still holding her jaw, though, and we're only an inch apart when our eyes open and lock in on one another's.

"Do you have a car here?" she whispers, eyes hooded with need.

I shake my head once. "You?"

"No."

"I can order a car. I don't live too far from here."

The fire in her eyes blazes a little hotter. "Okay."

I release her and pull my phone from my pocket.

"I'm going to gather up my stuff and tell my friends. Meet me by the front door?" She offers a smile before standing and walking away.

I watch her go. I watch the way her rounded ass sways from side to side. As she goes, she unties that flannel shirt from around her waist, only giving me a better view for a moment. Before she's out of my view, she's pulling her arms through to put the shirt back in its rightful place.

I quickly order a car and see that it will be here within a couple of minutes. I make my way to the bar and settle my tab, getting my card back before heading down the steps. I move directly for the front door. Sliding my hands into my pockets, I wait to see if she joins me. Part of me wonders if her friends will talk her out of this. I mean, it's dangerous to leave a club with a stranger you just met. But again, it's a common occurrence and has been for decades. At least these days, we have the security of modern day technology. I'm sure she has friends and family tracking her phone.

My lips pull up into a smile as she steps up in front of me. "Ready to go?"

"Let's do it." She wraps her hand around my arm, and the two of us step out into the night together.

The car I ordered is already parked against the curb, so I open the door for her, and she slides into the seat. I climb in behind her, and the car is off, carrying us through the busy Chicago streets, toward my penthouse apartment that's only a few blocks away.

"Do you live in the city?"

She nods. "Yeah, but I have a roommate." She glances at me. "You live alone?"

"I do."

Her eyes move to the windshield. "On the north side?"

I nod.

Her brows lift and fall as surprise paints her face. She leans back in the seat, crossing her arms over her chest as she keeps her eyes trained on the window. We're not touching, not talking. Every muscle tenses as I wonder what she could be thinking about. Is she having second thoughts? I guess this is always the most awkward part about leaving together, as you're just left waiting to get to the reason you left to begin with. What if the silence breaks the spell? What if she realizes she's making a mistake? There's always a chance of that happening, and there's only one way to find out.

The car parks against the curb of my building, and I open my door and climb out. I offer her my hand, and she takes it, so I help her out of the car and close the door behind us. The car drives off as she looks up at the building.

"You live here?"

"The top floor." I hold out my arm for her.

Her eyes move from the top of the tall building to mine, down to my arm. She bites her lower lip, and I'm left waiting to see if she's going to take my arm or if the ride was the key to breaking the spell.

KAYLEE

The butterflies in my stomach are fluttering their wings like crazy. His blue eyes make my blood boil, and my body warms. Remembering that kiss has every hair standing on end, and when I think of how good his hands felt on my body, my nerve endings sing, needing that high once again. Yes, I'm nervous about going home with a man I just met. Yes, I'm worried about how I'll feel tomorrow after sleeping with a man I don't know. But, at the same time, I feel like if I don't go through with this, I'll regret that decision in the morning. I could walk away right now, but I'll always look back on this night and wonder what could've happened.

I slide my arm through his, my fingers wrapping around his elbow as he leads the way to the entrance of the building. He puts in a quick, four-digit code, and then he's able to pull the door open. I'm surprised when I don't see a doorman standing guard, but maybe it's due to the late hour. The lobby of the building is nice. All floor-to-ceiling windows, tinted glass, marble floors, and a big, black chandelier in the center of the room. The elevators are on a shiny, black marble wall. He pushes the matte black button, and the matching elevator doors open as a bell rings.

Stepping into the small space, he hits the button for the top floor, causing the doors to close before we're starting to move up.

"You've only lived here a week?"

"That's right." He slides his hands into his black dress pants.

"Where'd you live before?" I ask, leaning my back against the wall.

He leans against the wall opposite of me, his eyes raking up my body slowly. "A little bit of everywhere, I guess. New York, mostly."

The elevator doors open, and he motions for me to step out. When I do, he leads the way down the hall toward what I'm assuming is his door. He pulls his keys from his pocket and unlocks it quickly. Then he steps into the dark apartment first, flipping on a light. I walk in behind him, taking the place in.

It's nothing like the apartment I live in. This place is big and open, with high ceilings. The same floor-to-ceiling windows the lobby has take up an entire exterior wall, so you get a beautiful view of the city below.

"Please, make yourself at home."

I set my purse on the entryway table where he's unloading his pockets. Walking toward the glass wall, I unbutton my shirt as I take in the city lights. I hear him walk across the floor, and I feel him when he comes to a stop behind me, even though he doesn't reach out and touch me.

"It's beautiful, isn't it?"

I nod. "It really is." I turn to face him.

His blue eyes move from the window over to me. "Can I get you a drink?"

I nod. "Sure."

I watch him walk to a drink cart, where he gets to work on making us a round of drinks. I pull my flannel off and have a seat on his black leather couch, continuing to take in the room until he walks over with a drink in each hand. I take the one he offers me, and then he sits at my side. I watch as he picks up the remote on the table. Pushing a button, a fire roars to life in front of us.

I take a large gulp of my drink, feeling my nerves starting to double. When he looks over at me, I can't stop the words from rushing from my mouth.

"I've never done this before."

His brows lift in surprise.

"I mean, I've had sex before, but I've never had sex with someone I just met like this."

He nods. "I understand. It's okay if you've changed your mind." He sets his drink down on the table, turning his full attention to me.

I shake my head. "No, I don't want to change my mind. I just …" I shrug. "I feel awkward, and I figured if I feel awkward, I probably look awkward, and I wanted to let you know why. It's not you."

"Noted." He nods. "But you don't have to do anything you don't want to do. I won't be upset. We can sit here and have this drink, and then …" He shrugs. "The rest is up to you. If you want to continue with our plans, great. If not, I'll order you a car to take you home."

I lean forward, setting my glass down on the table. "I'm not changing my mind," I tell him. I lift my knee and swing it around him until I'm sitting on his lap. His blue eyes lock with mine, and I watch them become darker as the need inside him grows.

"Are you sure about this?"

I nod, and the second I do, he's smashing his mouth to mine. His hands move to my outer thighs, and they slide up to my hips, pulling my dress with them. Now that it's bunched up around my waist, he pulls me down against him. I roll my hips, grinding against his hardness. "Mmmmm," he moans against my lips, kissing me harder and faster.

His hands seem to be everywhere all at once. They move from my hips up my back and downward once again. Suddenly, he grabs my dress at my waist, and he starts pulling it up my body. Our kiss breaks when he tugs it over my head; then I watch his eyes fully take me in.

"I knew you'd be fucking perfect," he mutters, pulling my mouth back to his.

His hands continue to explore, and my hips keep rocking. Our mouths stay welded together, and I start unbuttoning his shirt. The second I unfasten the last button, he's ripping his shirt off, and he's standing up, holding me against him all in the same motion. The next thing I knew, he's carrying me through his apartment. My eyes don't open until I feel him lay me down on something soft. I look around to find myself in what must be his bedroom.

I'm in the center of a large, king-size bed. There are a dozen throw pillows, and the blanket beneath my back feels as soft as silk. My eyes find his as he stands before me. I watch as he unfastens his belt, the metal clanking before the sound of him undoing his zipper hits my ears.

I wet my lips, watching the way his muscles are rippling with his movements. He's nothing short of perfect with his broad shoulders, toned biceps, flexing pecks, narrowed stomach, and tight six pack. I take in every glorious inch of him, my blood burning hotter when I see the V between his hips—the point disappearing below his white boxer briefs. I can see the outline of his manhood as it strains against the fabric. He appears to be large, massive, even in girth. Those butterflies start trying to escape again, tickling every nerve ending and pushing me to want more.

He doesn't push his boxers over his hips, though. Instead, he grabs my ankle and lifts my foot. He places the bottom of my boot against his hip, his fingers quick to untie and loosen the laces. He pulls off the boot and drops it onto the floor. It lands with a solid thud. Then his fingertip slips beneath my sock, and he's pulling it off, dropping it next to my boot. He repeats the process with my other foot before he puts his knee on the bed to climb up.

My legs are already spread for him, my knees bent and in the air as he takes his place between them. I sit up, lacing my fingers into his hair and pulling his mouth to mine for a hard, deep kiss. His tongue twists with mine as his hands slide around to my back. One quick flick of his fingers has my bra falling from my chest. He lays me back, and he pulls his lips from mine. He kisses his way down my body, his lips causing tiny little fires to spread across my flesh.

His hands cup my breasts. He pushes them together, and he massages them as his mouth kisses and sucks and bites at my mounds. He runs his tongue across my nipple, making it harden before moving on to the other. His hands stay in place, but his mouth moves lower, over my ribcage, down my stomach, and to my hip, where his teeth scrape against my skin.

My back arches off the bed when his face moves between my legs. He inhales my scent, and his hands finally move from my breasts. They move to cup my ass instead.

"Theo," I beg, my hands fisting the blanket beneath us.

He hasn't pulled down my panties yet, but somehow, he knows exactly where I need his touch because he scrapes his teeth against my cotton-covered center. His hot breath washing over my folds makes me feel like a flood has just slammed into me.

"You smell so sweet." He kisses my inner thigh. "I just want to eat you up."

"Please," I beg, feeling like my body will explode if I don't get some kind of relief.

His finger moves into the side of my panties, perfectly placed to slide deep inside of me. It feels so good to finally be touched, but it's not nearly enough. It's only enough to make me want him that much more.

"Theo, I ..." the words fall from my lips.

"What's the matter, gorgeous?"

My breathing is getting heavier and heavier with my excitement. I nearly pant out, "I need you." More labored breaths. "I need to—" My words fail when he rips my panties away and sucks my clit into his hot mouth. I'm immediately pushed over the edge, my orgasm ripping through me.

My back arches off the bed, and a loud moan slips from my lips. My legs try to close, but with his head between them, they just trap him right where I need him. My hands are fisting the blankets, holding myself down. I'm sure the amount of oxygen I'm sucking in right now would surely cause me to float away.

My toes curl. My knees shake. My eyes roll to the back of my head, and my heart is slamming against my chest so hard it may just bust through completely. I can't fight against the sensation holding me prisoner. All I can do is give into it, let it take me away like I'm nothing but a small boat in the middle of the ocean on a stormy night. The waves pick me up and throw me from here to there, and even though there's destruction, it's beautiful because now I know what it's like to be claimed by him.

My ride ends, and I melt into the bed. He doesn't pull away until he's sure I've had my fill. My eyelids feel heavy, but I manage to open them as he wipes my arousal from his lips with the back of his arm.

On his knees, his hands move to the waistband of his boxers. The fire in his dark blue eyes seems to be burning out of control as he looks down at me. "I hope you're not done with me yet." He pushes his boxers down his hips, and his long, hard cock springs free, bouncing up and down with excitement beading up on his tip.

I greedily look him up and down, and I lick my lips, more than ready for him to take what he wants because I know that process will only have him giving in return.

His hands start on my knees, which are still in the air on either side of him, and they slide down my thighs as he lowers himself onto me. My hand fists his dark hair, and I pull his mouth to mine, where my tongue thrusts into his mouth with just as much excitement as before. His cock is resting against my center, and I love the way his silky, soft skin feels against my sensitive folds.

"Do you still want this?" he whispers against my lips.

"God, yes," I breathe out, my hips wiggling to feel him slide against me.

He doesn't reply as he reaches between us. Positioning himself at my entrance, his hands squeeze my hips as he slides into me slowly. I gasp when I feel his thick cock spreading my walls. He breaks our kiss, but he doesn't pull away as our eyes open, staring into each other's as he slowly pushes deeper.

"Tell me when to stop," he whispers, softly kissing my lips.

I shake my head. "Don't stop."

He pulls his hips back, and he sends them flying into me again, this time moving deeper. I dig my nails into his skin as I stifle a scream. He's easily the largest I've ever been with. In fact, he may be too large, as I feel like I'm painfully stretching around him.

"Is it too much?" he asks, his voice shaky as his hands squeeze tighter on my hips.

I bite my lower lip as I open my eyes, locking them on his. "I like it," I confess in a whisper. "Just … go slow."

He pulls back and thrusts forward again. This time, I do call out, and that causes him to cover my mouth with his. While I'm feeling pain and pressure down below, his mouth is soft and sweet, almost like he's trying to make up for any pain he's causing. He may be stretching me to fit him, but it's like he's scratching an itch I didn't know I had.

Holding my hips in his hands, he rocks against me again and again. The longer he's inside of me, the more my body loosens around him. The pain eases away, turning into nothing but blinding pleasure, and before I know it, he's thrusting into me so hard and deep that the headboard is banging off the wall, and I can't do anything but hold onto him as he pushes my body to go spiraling once again.

"How rough do you like it, beautiful?" he whispers in my ear as he's sliding into me from behind.

I look over my shoulder at him, and he grins. Gathering my hair in one hand, he wraps it around his fist, causing the fire in his eyes to burn hotter, and I know this is a night I'll never forget.

THEO

Flawless. Exquisite. Life-changing.

I knew the second our eyes met in the club that she was the definition of perfection, and I was right. Everything about her has me drowning in amazement. Her eyes, I get lost in them, and I don't care if I ever find my way out. Her soft, plump lips, they're sweet and taste of vanilla and cinnamon. Her skin is like cashmere, and she smells of warmth and sunshine. Everything about her face pulls you in, causing you to be stunned by her angelic beauty. But her body … that's nothing but sin on top of sin, ready to tease, torture, and lead you to hell. And I fell into that trap. I don't care if I'm on the pathway to hell. Who knew hell could feel so good? With a face as beautiful as hers and a body that the devil created himself, she's the perfect storm.

She's tall and thin, but she has soft curves and hard lines. Her breasts slightly overfill my hands, but I love watching the way her flesh bubbles up between each of my outstretched fingers. I love the way she spills over the sides and how her nipples harden against my palms. Her stomach is toned and flat, slightly narrowing, so she has an hourglass figure. Her belly button is barely a little slit, almost almond shape. Her hips are slightly wider, with a soft curve that leads me down to the junction between her sexy thighs. She's hairless, soft, tight, and, oh, so responsive. All I have to do is look at her to make her pussy blush and glisten with arousal. My body is begging for a release, but I'm nowhere near ready to be done with her just yet.

I want to make her scream for me. I want her to beg for more, and then I want her begging me to stop. I want her entire body shaking from having me between her thighs. I want to make her mine in every way possible. I don't know if I'll ever see her again, but I know I want her looking back on this night for the rest of her life. I want to be the one who got away, the one who, if she ever ran in to me again, she'd leave her weak ass husband for me because I'm the only one who could ever fuck her right. I want her to feel me between her legs with every movement she makes for the next week. And even though she'll be sore, I want that soreness to make her wet her panties with a need that only I can fill.

Her hair is wrapped around my fist as I thrust into her greedy pussy as deep as I can go. I roll my hips while my fingers tease her clit, pushing her closer and closer to her breaking point. She's breathless, whimpering, and moaning. Her body is shaking, her muscles confusing. Her toes are curling, and goosebumps are prickling her skin. All it takes is one last roll of my hips before we're both falling over the edge. My body takes on a life of its own, thrusting faster, deeper, harder as I chase after every beautiful second of my orgasm.

My body is weak, tired, and breathless when I fall onto the bed at her side. My eyes shut as I do everything I can to get myself put back together, but the bed feels too good. The cool air feels amazing to my overheated skin. As my breathing slows, so does my heart, and before I know it, I'm out to the world.

* * *

My eyes open, finding the room filling with early morning light. I roll my head to the side, wanting to go back to sleep. I don't know what day it is or what time it is, but I'm tired enough that I could sleep for a week. What in the hell did I do last night to make me black out like I did? Did I have too much to drink?

My eyes pop open when memories of last night wash over me. Going to the club and meeting … What was her name? Shit, I better remember it before I have to address her.

My head turns back, finding the bed empty. I look at the bathroom door, finding it open with no light on. My head falls back against the pillow, and my eyes shut. Her green eyes fill my mind. I remember their almond shape. How she had long, black lashes. How her eyes were dark green around the rims and how they got lighter and brighter toward the center.

"Kay, " I whisper her name, and my eyes open again. "Kay?" I call out, but there's no answer. My bedroom door is closed, though. Maybe she's in the kitchen, making a cup of coffee, or finding something to eat. I push myself to get out of bed. I walk across the room naked, stopping at my dresser and opening the drawer to pull out a pair of sweatpants. In the bathroom, I relieve myself, and I wash my hands before venturing into the rest of the house to find her.

It's not until I walk into the living room, finding it empty, that it hits me. I didn't notice any of her things in the bedroom. I remember taking off her bra, her panties, socks, and boots in my room, yet none of them grabbed my attention. Now that I'm in the living room, I look at the couch as I remember taking off her dress there. Still, there's no dress, but there are two glasses on the coffee table.

She woke up early and left. Or she waited for me to pass out last night, and she left. Either way, she's gone, and I'm alone. I let out a long breath as I collapse onto the couch. My arm covers my eyes as I relax into the leather that's cool to my skin. I've wished for this to happen in the past, after meeting a woman at the club and bringing her home for some fun. We'd wake up the next morning, and I could see her trying to dig her claws into me. It was always awkward having a conversation the morning after, especially when I had to ask them to leave. The thing is, I didn't want Kay to leave. Not yet, anyway. It would've been nice to wake up to her at my side. We could have taken a shower together, touched, kissed. I wouldn't mind taking her for another ride.

Now she's gone, and I have no idea how to get ahold of her. We didn't exchange numbers last night. Hell, I didn't even get her last name. I have no idea where she lives or works. I guess the only thing I can do is go back to that club and hope to bump into her again. If I ever see her again, I will get her number. I'll make sure I know how to get ahold of her in the future because the two of us coming together last night was too perfect not to ever experience it again.

I guess I dozed back off as I lounged on the couch because I jump awake when my phone rings. I grab it from the table and bring it to my ear without even really looking at the screen. "Hello?"

"Hey, man. I didn't wake you, did I? It's almost twelve o'clock," Asher says.

"What? No, no, you didn't wake me. I was just reading. What's up?"

"I thought I'd see if you were busy. I was just about to head out to the country club for a round of golf. Thought you might want to join. We can have a few drinks, get some lunch, and catch up without any women interrupting. What do you think?"

I rub the sleep from my eyes as I push myself up. "Yeah. That sounds great. Send me the address, and I'll meet you there."

He sends me the address in a text, and I manage to get myself up off the couch. I take a quick shower and get dressed. By the time I'm pulling up at the country club, it's going on to one o'clock, so a late lunch it is. I'm approaching the doors when Asher steps up to my side.

He offers a smile as he pulls open the door for me. "They won't let you in without a membership card, so I waited for you out here so I could be sure you'd get in."

"Thanks for the invitation. I've been working so much; I could use some time away."

We step into the lobby of the country club, and he slides his hands into his pockets and nods. "No problem. If you like the place, we'll get you your own membership. Then you'll always have a place to escape to."

The hostess steps up to the counter, and Asher hands over his membership card that she swipes. I'm busy taking in the place while they exchange pleasantries. When they finish, I follow along behind him to the restaurant. I'm not surprised to see white tablecloths on every table, and nearly all of them are full. It seems this is a popular place to come if you're looking to have a business meeting, as several of the tables are filled with men wearing expensive suits. Several also hold nothing but older ladies who are enjoying their sandwiches and tea. Then, of course, there are the golfers and the tennis players.

It seems walking through gets most people's attention, as they all glance up at us as we pass. The women all smile at me, wave, or bat their eyelashes. I smile and nod, say hello when it's needed, but I tend to keep my eyes straight ahead like I don't notice them. If this is a place I want to visit to relax, I don't need any of these women thinking that I'm single or interested in them.

The hostess walks away from the table after dropping our menus on the top. Asher takes his seat, and then I unbutton my jacket before sitting across from him. He picks up his glass of water and chuckles, getting my attention.

"Do you feel like the new kid that started school halfway through the year?"

My brow lifts as I pick up my menu. "More like the newest exhibit at the zoo."

He grins. "It seems you have everyone's attention. Hey, you're single. I can tell you who to avoid if you want. A few of these ladies have been passed around, if you know what I mean." His eyes double in size.

I laugh. "No, thank you. I don't plan on becoming friends with any of them, let alone sleeping with them."

His brows furrow, and he rolls his eyes. "What happened to my best friend, who had to try for all the women? If I wasn't married, there are a few I wouldn't mind taking out to dinner." He glances around the room with a smirk.

The waitress comes over, and she sets two glasses of whiskey down. "Your usual, Mr. Jax."

"Thank you, Isabella." He picks up his glass and slips her a twenty. She walks away, and he motions for me to join him for a drink.

I pick up the glass and hold it in the air.

"To us, our long friendship, and to our future."

I tap my glass against his, and then we both take a sip.

"So …" Asher says, leaning back in his chair and crossing one leg over the other. "What's been going on in that life of yours? You still seeing Lena? Was that her name?"

I wave my hand through the air. "God, no. That lasted all of two minutes." I shrug. "I've been focusing on work. I can't even tell you the last time I had a date."

He frowns and scoffs. "I can't see you, Mr. Player, going that long without a woman in his life."

"It's true. Up until last night, I—"

His brow raises as he leans forward. "Whoa … Wait a minute. What happened last night? You were at my place last night."

I nod and take a sip. "I was. I stopped at a club on my way home—a spur-of-the-moment thing."

He nods. "A club? What are you? Twenty-two?" He laughs.

I chuckle and shrug. "Again, it was a spur-of-the-moment kind of thing. It wasn't planned. I walked in there and immediately knew it wasn't my kind of place, but I told myself to have a drink and give it a shot." I grin. "And boy, am I glad I did."

"Yeah?"

I nod, my grin only growing in size. "I met this woman there … Fucking perfect in every way."

His head falls back as he rolls his eyes. "Give me all the details. I've been married for a few years now. I have to live through you." He laughs.

"I mean …" I pull my eyes from his. "I'm not going to give you all the gory details, but …" Our eyes meet again. "We had a good time. I took her back to my place, and she was gone before I woke up this morning."

He shakes his head. "What's she look like?"

My heart begins to race as I picture her. "Gorgeous. Long dark hair, thin, but she also had plenty of curves to enjoy, and they were in all the right places." Even though I'm barely glossing over her description, I have a perfect view of her in my head. I picture her completely naked and lying before me with her legs spread, begging me to take her. I remember how soft her skin was under my hands, how her perky tits bounced each time I thrust into her, how hot and tight she felt wrapped around my dick.

I have to shake the mental image from my head when my body starts to tingle and come alive. I grab my glass of whiskey, and I bring it to my lips, finishing it off and using the burn to kill the sensations that's tingling in my gut.

"It sounds like this woman really got under your skin." He watched me gulp down the whiskey and now that my glass is gone, he's looking at me with amusement.

I shrug and wet my lips. "That's not always a bad place to be, I guess."

He smirks. "No, I guess it's not." He finishes off his glass, and then he's flagging down the waitress and motioning for another round. This time, we both order some lunch. We sit and eat, talk, and catch up. When we're finished with lunch, we head out to play a round of golf.

KAYLEE

The alarm goes off annoyingly early on Monday morning. I jump awake, aimlessly smacking at the clock on my bedside table to silence it. In the process, I knock it from my table, but at least the sound has stopped. My head falls back against my pillow, my heart racing like I've just escaped a masked murderer.

I'm so not ready for this—it's too early. Not to mention, I really don't want to have to look at Travis. Things ended with us months ago, but we've only seen one another a handful of times since the night I broke up with him. Every time I did see him, though, he looked at me with every emotion on his sleeve. I saw hurt and pain in his eyes. I saw anger and betrayal. Now I have to see him today and pretend like I don't notice how much I hurt him. A sigh slips from my lips because putting it off isn't going to make it any better. I may as well get up and embrace the day ahead.

I push back my blankets, and I sit up, stretching and rolling my stiff neck before standing and moving toward the door. The moment I step into the hallway, the delicious smell of coffee and cinnamon washes over me, and I inhale it deeply. I'm so lucky that my roommate is a morning person. Now, I'll be able to reward myself for getting ready with a big cup of coffee and whatever that sweet smell is before starting my day.

I take a quick shower and then finish getting ready in my room. I grab my bag and rush toward the kitchen, where Margo is already sitting at the table with a cup of coffee and a pan full of cinnamon rolls. She looks up at me with a grin. "I figured you'd be hungry."

"It smells so good. Tell me you made those from scratch," I say, pouring my coffee.

"Is there any other way?"

I quickly take my coffee back to the table and sit across from her. She's already plating up one of the giant cinnamon rolls and sliding it across the table.

I pull the plate closer with one hand while the other reaches for the roll, picking it up and moving it toward my mouth, even though the icing is melting and drizzling onto the plate. I take a big bite, and my eyes fall closed as the feeling of heaven takes me away. "Mmmmmm."

She laughs. "I don't think they're *that* good. It sounds like you're getting off over there," she teases.

My eyes open, and I roll them as I lick the icing from my upper lip. "Screw it. I'll do it."

"Do what?" She frowns.

"I'll drop down on my knee right now and ask you to marry me."

She scoffs.

"Honestly, I don't know why you haven't already been snatched up. Do these boys know what they're missing?" I point my index finger at her. "No, that's it. You're dealing with boys. If a man knew how perfect you were, you would've been married off long ago."

She sits back in her chair, smiling and shaking her head. "Well, thank you for stroking my ego. Keep it up, and I may just accept that marriage proposal." She playfully winks at me, making me giggle around a mouthful of cinnamon roll.

"Now, onto a more serious topic of discussion: We're all meeting up outside the gym this morning."

It feels like my shoulders cave in on myself. "Not this already," I whine, stomping my foot under the table.

"Hey, you knew this was going to happen when school started back up. And you knew the dangers of dating someone on the football team to begin with."

I sip my coffee. "You're not wrong. I just didn't know that a member of the football team would take it so hard. Every time I see him, I just feel guilty all over again. He acts like I ran over his puppy or something."

She chuckles. "Well, you broke his heart."

I level my eyes on her. "What would you have done? He was already making plans for when we graduated. He wanted us to get married, live together, and start our careers. He was even talking about where we'd go on our honeymoon and how many kids we'd have." I point at my chest while shaking my head. "I can't even decide what I want for dinner tonight, let alone think about marriage and kids. Breaking up with him was the right thing to do. Yes, he was already attached, but it could've been much worse if I waited." My eyes fall down to my plate as I gently shake my head. "He knew when we started dating that I wasn't looking for marriage or kids any time soon. He knew I wanted to focus on my writing career."

I look up when I feel her placing her hand over mine.

"You did the right thing, sis. I would've done exactly what you did; only you did it with so much more class and grace than I ever would have. I wouldn't have spent the summer avoiding everyone keeping from reminding him that he lost me. I would've been out there, living my best life. He'll get over it eventually. Don't let him make you feel guilty for being true to yourself for another minute. Got it?"

I can't help it, but her speech put a smile on my face. I nod and squeeze her hand back. "Thank you."

"Now, finish up. We need to get to campus so we can start planning the first party of the year." She stands up, taking her plate and cup to the sink to clean up.

The first party of the year is always thrown by the football team after the first game of the season. The cheerleaders always help plan the event, and it's always the biggest and best party of the year. This is a yearly tradition that can't be broken. It was started long before us, and it will go on long after us. Sure, if I don't participate, I'm sure nothing will change, but I don't want to rob myself of any experiences this year. It's my senior year—the last year of being a kid, for lack of a better term. Next year, I'll be holding down a career. I won't be focusing on parties or having fun. I'll be a contributing member of society.

I finish with my breakfast, and I clean up. Margo and I grab our things, and we head out together for our last first day of school. We don't live too far from campus, and since the weather is still nice, we walk the four blocks instead of driving in rush hour traffic. On campus, we grab a coffee from the coffee cart, and we meet up with our group outside of the gym as planned. For the first few minutes, everyone just stands around, greeting one another and catching up. Travis walks up late, but our eyes find one another the second he does.

I can see the change in him the moment he realizes that I'm still here, a part of this group. He went from looking just fine to looking upset and sad. He tucks his hands into his jean pockets, and his shoulder bows inward slightly. His back is hunched forward, his stance making him look smaller and weaker than he really is.

He looks good, though. His brown hair is combed, looking soft and freshly cut into his retro feathered style. Last time I saw him, the back of his hair was nearly to his shoulders. Now, it's up off his neck, but still long and shaggy as it covers his ears and frames his face.

He pulls his brown eyes from mine as he exchanges high fives and fist bumps with the guys. "Let's get this started. I need to get to class on time," he says to the group, figuratively tapping the gavel that gets this meeting started.

I stand back with the other cheerleaders, listening as everyone volunteers to handle a different area of the party. The guys plan on getting the kegs and liquor along with the band. The girls talk entertainment, invites, and decorations. I give up nothing. I'll help if I'm asked to, but if I'm not, I don't plan on getting my hands dirty with it. I thought I wanted to be just as involved as everyone else, but now that I'm here, surrounded by everyone, I feel like I've grown and changed over the summer while everyone else has stayed exactly the same.

The meeting wraps up, and everyone starts to go their own way. Margo waves goodbye, and just as I'm about to turn and walk toward my first class, Travis steps in front of me, blocking my path. My feet stop moving, and I look up at him. "Hey." I force a smile.

"You have a minute to talk?"

I tighten my hand that's holding the shoulder strap of my bag. "Sure. What's up?"

He takes a deep breath, and his hand combs through his hair. I watch as it all falls back into its rightful place. "I just wanted you to know that you don't have to keep avoiding me."

"I haven't—" I start, but he cuts me off.

"You have. I've barely seen you all summer, and I know that's because of our breakup. I'm not over it." His eyes fall to the ground between us. "I don't know if I'll ever be over it, but I know we both have to move on." He looks at me now. "You're a hard one to get over, Kaylee."

I offer him a smile. "Thanks, Trav."

He nods as he takes a few steps back. He looks me up and down once more before finally turning and walking away.

I take a deep breath, preparing to push forward, when Xander steps in front of me. He's wearing a wide smile, and his blue eyes are shining. "How'd that go?"

"How'd what go?"

He glances over his shoulder toward Travis, who's still walking away but in our line of sight.

I shrug. "Fine, I guess. How's he been doing this summer? I hope I didn't hurt him too much."

He waves his hand through the air. "Don't worry about him. He's a big boy. He's going to have to learn to get over it and let things go when they end."

I feel my brows raise out of surprise. I thought the whole team would hate me as much as Travis does.

"Listen … Now that you're single again, and Trav says he's over the whole breakup thing …"

I cross my arms over my chest. "Are you asking me out?"

He chuckles and runs his hand through his short, blond hair. "I mean, I'm trying to."

I shake my head. "Isn't that going against the *bro-code* or whatever?"

He rolls his eyes. "Yeah, it would be if Trav didn't give me his permission."

"He gave you permission?" Shock washes over me.

He nods. "Yeah, right after you two broke up. I waited for the summer just so I didn't seem like a dick, but now …"

A scoff slips from my lips. I don't bother shaking my head or verbally answering him. I just walk past, heading to class. He doesn't even try to stop me, but I know this isn't over. He's just now starting to lay the groundwork. He'll keep at it, asking again and again and again. He'll flirt and show me more attention than any other girl at the parties. I know because I've seen him do it before. Every girl in this school is interested in Xander. He could ask any of them out, and they'd all say yes. So why did he have to pick me?

My morning classes pass quickly, and luckily enough, most of my professors take it easy on us with it being the first day of class. I have a few assignments to do tonight, but nothing that I'm downright dreading. Maybe if I'm lucky, I'll get another week of being assignment-free before real life kicks in and they start drilling us with work.

I sit with Margo and a few of the girls at lunch. They're all excited about the party, and they're already in party-planning mode. They run their ideas by me, and I either nod along or dismiss them, but I don't give them much help when it comes to suggestions. Really, I don't know why they try so hard. Every year, it's always the same. The living room is always the video game, talk, and hangout room. The kitchen is where the football team hangs out, so they can guard all the alcohol. The backyard will have a bonfire, and the game room in the basement will be the dance/make-out area. Really, the only thing that ever changes about this party is the theme. My freshman year, the theme was the classic toga party. My sophomore year, it was a luau. Last year, we did a Bonnie and Clyde theme. And it seems like this year we'll be having a cops-and-robbers-themed party. The girls are already talking about who is going to be what and how they're going to take the cops and robbers theme and make it fun and adult.

Throughout lunch, I find myself drifting off, not wanting anything to do with the party or this conversation. Maybe it's a good thing that this is my last year. It seems like I'm outgrowing all this college, party-life stuff. Last year, I was just as involved as these girls. This year, moving to New York and landing my dream job sounds better and better.

Luckily, lunch ends rather quickly, and I'm able to go to the rest of my afternoon classes, which keeps my mind off of Travis, our breakup, the party, and Xander. The final class for the day isn't really a class at all. It's making an appearance at the newspaper for our first meeting and to plan the first issue for the year.

Walking into the newsroom, I feel a little anxious because I was supposed to meet the instructor at my dad's dinner this past weekend, only I cancelled to go out with the girls. I smile to myself as I take my seat behind my usual computer desk, my thoughts going back to that night out—not so much the night out but leaving the club and how I ended up spending the night.

I shiver when a chill races up my spine, and my skin covers in goosebumps. I remember the way his blue eyes darkened, how silky his dark hair felt between my fingers when I fisted it. I take a deep breath, and somehow, the smell of his cologne washes over me, lighting a fire in my lower belly that's almost impossible to ignore.

"Everyone, I want you to meet our guest instructor, Theo Miller."

Everyone starts to clap, and I snap out of my daze, my eyes moving up to land on the man who's frozen in the doorway, blue eyes glued to mine. Our guest instructor ... Theo Miller ... My dad's friend, who I was supposed to meet over dinner last weekend ... happens to be the man I met at the club, the man who's bed I slept in, the man who knows my body better than even I do. And he looks just as surprised to see me as I am to see him.

THEO

I hear the student editor introduce me to the class, so I step into the room. I was shown around the newsroom earlier in the day, so I'm not busying myself with looking over the class I'll be in for the next year. I'm not impressed with the twenty-or-so top top-of-the-line computers—a donation, no doubt. I'm not even surprised by the number of students who work on the paper. What does catch me off guard is walking in and coming face-to-face with the woman I brought home from the club last weekend—the woman I haven't been able to stop thinking about. Since she's a returning member of the paper, she's taken the same desk she had last year. I look away from her shocked green eyes down to the paper taped to the front of her desk that reads: Kaylee Jax – Entertainment.

Kay … Kaylee. I should have known. I mean, there's no way I could have guessed that the woman I met and took home was the only daughter of a very old friend of mine. He's the only reason I'm even here. He offered me this job as a favor, and what have I done? I went and defiled his only daughter? It's one thing to hook up with a student. It's another when you fuck your best friend's daughter.

Getting introduced to the class, they all welcome me with a round of applause. I walked in with a smile on my face. That fell away the moment my eyes met hers. And now, the applause has faded away as well, and all I've been doing is staring at the woman in front of me, frozen in shock.

Her green eyes sweep from the left to the right, and her brows arch. When her eyes are back on mine, they widen, and I read the signal she's giving me. People are starting to stare and wonder what my problem is. I better do something fast if I don't want anyone putting two and two together.

So, I clear my throat and slide my hands into the front pockets of my pants. "Thank you for the very warm welcome, everyone." I push myself toward the editor's desk that sets at the front of the room, and I lean against it. "As Mr. Elder here said ..." I motion toward him. "I am the guest instructor for the year. Now, I know that in the past, the students have entirely run the newspaper, so some of you may not be too happy to learn that I'll be here this year, but I assure you, I do not plan on taking this paper from you. I don't plan on changing the way you do things around here. Nor do I plan on *teaching* in a way you'd expect. With all of this being said, you're probably wondering why I am here, and I'll tell you."

I stand from the desk as I start walking around the room. "Dean Harrison said that twenty-five years ago, being on the paper was a coveted spot. He said there were, at least, two hundred people a year applying to get a spot—a spot just like the one you all have." I wet my lips as I turn my attention to the class. "That number has gone down over the years, and that's to be expected. I mean, writing isn't something you start doing because you want to be rich or famous, right?"

I've made my way back to the front of the class, so I lean against the desk once again. "Writing isn't like taking any other office job. You can't pawn your work off on someone in the office to do. You can't fake talent. Writers are born. They are not made. It takes special people to not only survive but to succeed in a writing career. People have started to learn this, and so less and less are applying to be on the paper. Of course, we can always blame the modern times. These days, everything is online, so why pick up a paper? More and more people doing that means less and less papers to print, which shows in the decline of your print numbers over the years. So, while I may not be here to teach, exactly, I am here to get this program back on its feet.

"You may want to ask: What gives me the idea that I can turn things around? Well, I am the owner and creator of Suits Magazine for Men and Heels Magazine for Women."

The whole room gasps.

Throughout my speech, I've been avoiding her, but now I glance her way to see that her eyes have doubled in size.

"Whoa, aren't you like … a billionaire?" one of the students asks. "What are you doing here?"

"I'm actually friends with a professor here. He and I go back to our college days. We stayed in touch over the years, and when this position came available, he gave me a call because he thought, and the dean agreed, that having me here would set an example of how hard work can pay off even in a career that's hard to succeed in."

I hold up my finger. "I do want to say that over the course of this coming year, I do plan on working with each and every one of you to develop your writing skills. At the end of the year, don't be surprised if I offer someone a job to come to work for me in New York, writing for one of my magazines."

Everyone gasps and whispers sound like roars as they move through the room. I look back at Kay. She's resting her head on her fist, and her eyes are downcast. She doesn't look happy to have me here.

"Okay, okay," I say, quieting them down. "Let's go around the room and introduce yourselves so I can start learning some names." I point to the first person to my right.

The girl stands up, states her name, what year of school she's in, how long she's been writing, and what she writes. When she sets down, the guy next to her stands and starts with the same process. One after another introduces themselves to me, and I follow along to the best of my ability. It's not until she stands that I'm able to dedicate my full attention to the person who's talking.

"My name is Kaylee Jax. I'm a senior this year, and I've been a member of this paper since I started school my freshman year. I also dedicated four years of high school and three years of junior high school to my school papers. I'm writing entertainment this year, but I've done this for so long now that I've worked in every department." She takes her seat, and the guy next to her leans in.

The students keep telling me about themselves, but my attention is now on Kay and the guy she's talking to. He has his arm wrapped around the back of her chair as they talk quietly. They're both smiling, and I can tell by the way he's keeping her in his sights that he's interested in more than just her experience on the paper. Question is: Is she interested in him?

After everyone has been introduced, the editor of the paper moves to the head of the room, and he starts doing his job of handing out assignments. He directs the photographers to cover this week's cross country meet, the first football game of the season, and the girls' volleyball game, while our three sports writers are to go to the games and write their articles. Kaylee gets asked to interview a few members who are participating in the upcoming play, while other writers are asked to cover some of the student interest pieces and ongoings around campus.

I stand back and watch everything get assigned. After assignments are given, it seems like everyone goes in their own direction. The editor leaves, stating he needed to get to his part-time job. The photographers leave because they have no reason to be in class. And the writers, some stay to get to work while others take off, because when you're a writer, you can work from anywhere, as long as you have a computer and internet access.

I've always liked to stand back and watch the newsroom, find out who stays late and comes in early, because those are usually the ones who care the most. The class is almost empty when Asher walks in. His eyes find his daughter immediately, and he smiles.

"There she is. I take it the two of you have already met?"

Kay stands and moves in to hug her dad. "Hey, Dad. I'm really sorry about missing dinner last weekend."

He waves his hand through the air. "It's okay. I'm sure you really needed the rest."

Her face turns pink as Asher looks at me.

"So, did you two meet?"

"Not officially," I tell him, holding out my hand to her. "I'm friends with your father, if you can't tell." I laugh, and he gives her a wide smile.

"It's nice to meet you, professor." She slips her hand into mine, and all the butterflies I felt last weekend are back. My fingertips warm and tingle before shooting up my arm. I pull my hand away quickly, not needing to feel any sort of attachment to her.

"Please, just call me Theo. I'm not a professor."

She nods, but Asher rolls his eyes. "If anyone should be called professor, it's you. You're saving this program, you know?"

I slide my hands into my pockets. "I don't know about that. I guess we'll see."

"Have you gotten to read anything she's written?" he asks me while pointing at his daughter.

I shake my head. "No, not yet. We've only introduced ourselves, and the editor has handed out some assignments. I figured I'll just hang out in the back this week, see how things are done around here before making my mark. I'm sure I'll read something of hers next week when she submits for the paper." I smile as I glance at her.

She wets her lips and then swallows, her green eyes boring into mine.

I look from her to Asher, and I realize why her eyes looked so familiar the night we met. Asher's have gotten darker over the years, but she has his eyes. Hers are more vibrant than his have ever been. I feel like everything was staring me in the face, and I chose to ignore it. If I did, it wasn't a conscience decision that I remember making. The biggest mistake I made that night was meeting someone I knew was much younger than me and not asking if she goes to this university where I had just taken a job. If I knew then that she was a student here, I never would've taken her home.

"Well, I should gather my stuff and get home. I have plenty of homework that needs my attention," Kay says, pulling away from her father.

His hand falls from her shoulder back to his side. "Homework? On the first day?" He turns to look at her.

She's at her desk now, loading her things into her bag. "Yep, and I'll get more work done if Margo isn't home." She throws her bag over her shoulder. She rushes over, hugging her dad before telling both of us goodbye.

Now, Asher and I are the only ones left in the room.

"I'd buy you a beer to celebrate your first day on the job, but we're on campus. How about a cup of coffee from the cart outside?"

I laugh and nod. "Yeah, okay. Why not?"

The two of us leave the class and walk through the building, toward the exit. Along the way, he tells me where I can find his classroom and where Meredith's class is. When we exit the building, a gathering group steals both our attention. We walk past on our way to the coffee cart, but we both watch the football players and cheerleaders as they talk, laugh, and hang out. The group isn't what has my attention, and I'm sure it's not what is keeping his either. It's her, Kay. She's standing with them, a big smile on her face.

"I didn't like her cheering," Asher admits as we walk closer to the cart on the sidewalk.

"Why is that?" I ask, frowning, not liking the way that football player is inching closer to her.

We get to the cart, but there's a line, so we both stop. He turns so he's facing the group that's now twenty feet or more away from us. "You remember how the cheerleaders were back in our day?"

I smile wide. "Yes, I do." I remember hooking up with almost every one of them.

He nods. "Exactly. I wanted her to focus on her studies. Get good grades." He shrugs. "But we made a deal. She promised to keep her grades up in high school if I promised to keep my mouth shut and let her have her fun. As she pointed out, she's cheering when she could be out going to parties." He crosses his arms over his chest. "Anyway, she held up her end of the bargain, and so did I. Here she is, years later, still cheering."

We move up in line. "Well, that doesn't seem too bad."

"No, but I hate that she dates the football players. She just broke up with one before summer. Now it looks like there's another in line." He scoffs and shakes his head, finally turning his attention to the front of the line.

"There's always going to be someone in line, Asher," I tell him, but I can't take my eyes off her any more than he can, only for a very different reason.

I guess I can claim I'm being overprotective of my friend's daughter, but the truth is, I'm not. I don't look at her and see a weak girl who needs protection. I look at her and see a beautiful woman who showed me an amazing time last weekend—a woman I would die to touch again—a woman who took my world and shook it upside down. Watching her with that guy only makes me jealous. I'm better than him in a million different ways, yet she's forbidden for me while he's allowed to talk to her, flirt with her, touch her in front of everyone like this? Her green eyes land on mine, and I see the fire in them erupt. She bites her lower lip, and her chest starts to rise and fall a little quicker.

Maybe she can't stop thinking of our night together either. But knowing that will not make this any easier on me. Now, I feel more tortured than ever.

KAYLEE

His hands are on my hips. He's lifting me up and pulling me back down. I'm on the brink of release, my head back, mouth open, moans and whimpers pouring out of me without a care. When my eyes open and I look down at him, my release takes over, pumping through my body with speed and power. Seeing him is all it takes to push me over the edge. I love the way his eyes darken when he looks at me. It's like I can see the need bubbling up inside of him, like his eyes are the window that allows me to look in. His lips are slightly parted, and his brows are pulled together, causing two lines to form between them. His chest is rising and falling quickly, his breath heavy with excitement and exhaustion. His biceps are flexed as he lifts me up, his shoulders and pecks rock hard. His abs are flexed, and this time, when I notice the V between his hips, it's not cut off by his boxers but by my body, and the two of us are now one.

My eyes pop open, and I find myself in my dark bedroom. Alone.

I can't get him off my mind. I can't stop dreaming of him. Having to see him every day but being unable to talk to him, to touch him—it's torture. How did things end up this way? Today is the last day of school for the week, and he hasn't looked at me since Monday. He's avoided me all week long, and the more he avoids me, the more obsessed I become. Maybe obsessed isn't the right word. It gets a bad rap. Maybe I should say the more he avoids me, the more I want him. How is it so easy for him to resist looking at me? I tried it the first day, but I failed more times than I could count. He's not failing, and knowing that hurts. Maybe I meant nothing to him, but I find that hard to believe because when you experience what we experienced, it leaves its mark.

My eyes move to the clock to find that it's only 3 a.m. It's too early to get out of bed, but I feel wide awake, like my body is tingling with excited energy. Plus, what would I do at 3 a.m. anyway? Taking a deep breath, I roll to my side and force my eyes to shut. My mind goes back to last weekend, where I relive being inside his bedroom. I remember the way he looked down at my naked body and how he licked his lips, like he was ready to eat me up. My body engulfs in flames, imagining how he crawled up my body, how he touched me, how he kissed me, and tasted me. I remember how he manipulated my body, pushing me over the edge again and again and again.

I roll over and pull open the top drawer on my bedside table. Reaching to the very back, my hand wraps around the velvety, soft rose toy. Laying back, I position the toy between my legs and power it on. While the little toy gets to work, my mind goes back to that night, remembering his face being buried between my legs. The toy mixed with the memory of him; I'm coming undone in a matter of minutes. My release washes through my body strong, and I give myself over to it. I hold onto my orgasm as tight as I can for as long as I can. When it ends, I'm weak, tired, fulfilled. It's not long before I'm fast asleep, back to dreaming of him.

* * *

"Party tonight. You're coming, right?" Xander asks, putting his hand on the tree I'm leaning against.

My eyes move up to lock on his. I shrug. "Probably."

"Probably? This is the best party of the year. Nobody misses it."

I tear my eyes from his, looking off into the distance as I try and come up with an excuse to miss the party. Only … every last thought slips from my head when Theo comes into view. He's walking to class looking sexy as hell. His designer jeans fit him perfectly, and that white button-down reminds me of the night we met. The sleeves aren't rolled up to his elbows this time, but I'm sure that's because he's on the clock. I bet the minute he walks away from this place, he's rolling them up. Thinking about his arms only has me remembering what it felt like to have them wrapped around me. The butterflies in my stomach come alive, and my heart leaps to life.

He must feel me staring at him because he turns his head and his eyes meet mine. I see the icy blue warm as a fire erupts in them. His jaw flexes, and his hand turns to a fist at his side.

As quickly as that look appeared, he wipes it away. The fire has been extinguished, now replaced with anger, but what could he be angry about? He's the one who's avoided looking at me all week.

"Sorry, Xander, but I have to go." I slip out from under his arm, keeping my eyes trained on Theo as I follow him into class. He's too far ahead of me, though, so by the time I walk in, he's already deep in conversation with someone else. Feeling let down, I take my seat. I type my passcode into the computer, and I get to work on the article I'm writing. The newsroom is surprisingly busy today. I was hoping to get a few minutes alone with him, but it seems like so is everyone else. They want to talk to him, suck up, get themselves in line for that job he was talking about earlier in the week. I don't want him for his money or for some job that may or may not be available. I just want him to look at me the same way he did a week ago, before he found out who I was.

It's not mandatory that we write all of our assignments here in the newsroom, but it's always open for those who want to. Before, I only came in to get my assignments. I'd write and submit them from home, and I wouldn't come back until the next week. This week, I've been at this desk every single day just so I can be around him. I tell myself to be patient; he'll look at me one of these days. Hell, maybe we'll even talk since that's something we haven't really done yet—other than the few words we exchanged on the first day when my dad walked into the room. It's like there's a giant elephant in the room, and I know it will be there until we talk about the things we've done. He seems just fine, acting like it never happened, but I can't ignore that elephant when it's sitting right in front of my face.

I hang out behind my desk, working and pretending to work for at least an hour, hoping to get a moment alone with him, but it never happens. It's like the moment he's done talking with one student, another approaches. Just when I think I may have a chance, he decides to leave for the day.

Annoyed, I push my chair back and stand from my desk to gather my things. I can't believe I wasted an hour sitting here doing nothing when I could've been home, getting my homework done before the game tonight.

As I walk out of the class, I tell myself that I need to let him go. I need to move on. Forget about last weekend—he clearly has—and if he can forget about me, I will forget about him.

Back at home, I spend the little time I have left getting my homework done for the weekend. Then I eat and get my uniform on for the game. Margo and I make the walk over together, knowing we'll be going to the party right after—neither of us wanting to drive when we know we'll be drinking.

The game kicks off, and the girls and I do our job of cheering on the team and getting the crowd involved with keeping the spirits high. Between cheers, I take in the large crowd in front of me. My eyes sweep over every face as a tingle forms in my lower belly. The hair on the back of my neck stands up, and I'm unsure why. That is, until my eyes find his in the crowd. Theo is sitting next to my dad and Meredith. Everyone seems to be watching the game. Everyone but him. His eyes are on me, and suddenly it makes sense as to why I felt the electric current throughout my body. The minute our eyes lock, he quickly turns his attention back to the game, but the damage has already been done. I've already caught him staring.

We start up the next cheer, and instead of glancing around the stands, I keep my attention on him and him alone. I smile a little bigger. I bat my lashes a little more, and I swing my hips, just hoping to draw him in. It's all I can do when I'm trying to flirt with a guy who's a hundred feet away. Somehow, it does the job because I watch him as his eyes slowly slide back over to me. I do a high kick, and the fire in his eyes erupts, warming them from an icy blue to a deep, dark ocean water blue. His jaw flexes, and his Adam's apple bobs. His chest expands when he sucks in a deep breath—a breath he holds for a long moment, as his chest never falls back into place for as long as I'm watching.

I spin, bend, and snap back up with the end of the cheer. My smile widens, and I send him a flirty wink. The look on his face tells me that he's turned on. I know because it's the same way he looked at me just last weekend. But there's also some anger and annoyance before he redirects his eyes back to the game.

I guess some girls would be upset that he was able to look away, but I'm not. He's refused to look at me all week. He's finally giving in. Maybe I'm wearing him thin. Maybe he's getting tired of fighting. All I know is that this is progress. If he can slip once, he will slip again and again, and that's exactly what I need.

He and I haven't talked since the night we were together. We haven't discussed the things we've done or how we're connected. He hasn't told me that we have to stop, even though his actions have made that clear. But I want to tell him that we don't have to stop. We're both adults here, and I'm more than capable of making my own choices.

The game comes to an end, and I start to gather my things while the people in the stands start making their way toward the gates. I keep my attention on him from the corner of my eye. I see my dad looking my way. He holds his hands in the air and waves them like he's trying to land a plane. I know he's trying to get my attention. I know he's wanting to ask me to join him and Meredith for dinner—it's something he does every year after the first game—it's also something I like to avoid if at all possible. Theo is standing next to them still. He's looking at me just like my dad is, but before I can turn, I'm being picked up and thrown over someone's shoulder. A squeal slips out as my eyes focus on the giant number 12 on the back of the jersey.

Xander.

"Time for that party, Kay." He lands a firm smack to my ass.

All around us are the football team and the cheerleaders, all happy, cheering, and jumping up and down to celebrate the win. Yelling and screaming to be put down would be useless. I don't fight it. I just let myself get carried away with the rest of the team. I lift my head and look up to see my dad, who's now turning his back to me as he retreats, Meredith following.

But Theo, he hasn't moved. No, he's still standing place, eyes trained on me. His jaw is flexed, and his eyes are narrowed; two lines are forming between his brows. It doesn't take a genius to see the anger and jealousy on his face, and it's this exact moment when I know without a shadow of a doubt that I'm living inside his head, just as much as he's living inside mine.

He may be able to resist looking at me in class. He may be able to ignore me, but he cannot pretend that I don't exist. Even if he manages to keep me from his thoughts here in the real world, I'm running through every dream he has, every fantasy. As much as I want him, I now know that he wants me too.

Xander finally sets me on my feet next to the locker room door as the boys go rushing through. The girls surround me, all of them talking and giggling with excitement for the win and the after-party. In all the craziness going on, Theo and I are the only two who are perfectly still as we look at one another. There's a football field between us, but it's going to take a lot more than that to keep us apart.

A Note from the Author

> *"There is a charm about the forbidden that makes it unspeakably desirable."*
>
> — *MARK TWAIN*

Let's keep Kaylee and Theo apart a moment longer, shall we? Have you ever felt that feeling? That electric tension when you realize that you're on the mind of the person you desire just as much as they're on yours? Once that shadow of doubt is removed from your thinking, it's like you can lean into the rawness of everything you feel. You know you're exposing yourself to being hurt, but you don't care: They're all you want ... and now you know that they want you too.

You either know that feeling, or you want to know it. Without breaking you away from the story too much, that's why we like to read romance, and when that romance is forbidden, it makes it all the hotter. I'd even go so far as to guess that when you've finished this book, you'll be hungry for more. You might even go on to read reviews of other forbidden romance novels, looking for your next fix.

Right now, someone else is doing the same thing, and you can help them find the story of Kaylee and Theo by leaving a review of your own.

By leaving a review of this book on Amazon, you'll help other readers who are looking for their next fix find exactly the romance they're looking for.

I won't keep you any longer. You're eager to get back to the story, I know. Thank you for your support, and somewhere —maybe on the other side of the world—there'll be another reader thanking you too.

Scan the QR code below

THEO

"Well, I guess she won't be joining us for dinner after all," Asher says as we all watch her get carried across the field by one of the players.

Meredith looks up at her husband. "Let her be. You know there's always a party after the first home game, and since they won, it will probably be extra crazy. It's her senior year. Let her have some fun."

Asher looks back to me. "I guess it's just the three of us then."

I do my best to offer a smile. "Thanks, but I'm afraid I'll have to take a raincheck. I'm just not feeling up to dinner tonight. I think I'm going to go home and call it a night."

"You sure?" Asher asks, quirking his brow as if he's studying me.

I nod. "Next time, my friend." I hold out my hand to shake.

He slaps his into mine, and after we shake, he turns and leads his wife away, leaving me standing in place. I can't stop myself from turning and looking across the field for her. I find her immediately, our eyes locking even with this massive field between us. It's almost like we're somehow in tune. Normally, this wouldn't be a bad thing, but in our case, it is. She's my student. She's my best friend's daughter. She's forbidden, but I want her like I've never wanted anyone before. I've managed to keep my eyes to myself, for the most part, this past week, but that didn't keep her off my mind. She consumes almost all of my thoughts, and when I forcefully push her from my head, she sneaks back in the moment I fall asleep.

She's calling to me, and I don't know how long I can resist her. This pull she has on me only seems to get stronger every day. I know it's only a matter of time before I'm too exhausted to fight. I know I'll end up giving in just so we can both get what we want. That look in her eyes tells me that she wants me just as much right now as she did the night we met. She doesn't care about all the ways that make this wrong. Deep down, I wish I could be more like her.

I rip my eyes away, and I turn to leave the field. Now that the crowd has died down, it's easier and faster to get to the gates. I climb behind the wheel of the car I'm leasing, and I make the drive back to my place. The moment I enter, I light a fire. I kick off my shoes and change out of my day clothes and into something more comfortable for relaxing. Once I have my sweatpants and a Henley on, I pour myself a stiff drink and have a seat in front of the warm fire. My skin is a little cool from being at the game after dark for the last couple of hours. It absorbs the much-needed heat that warms my bones and causes my tense muscles to finally relax.

I take a sip of the whiskey in my glass, swallowing it down while melting into the couch. Just like any other time when my mind isn't occupied, it goes back to thinking of her and the night we spent together. I think about how she sat here next to me, how she climbed onto my lap and pressed her lips to mine. I remember the way her heat sunk into my body and how good her weight felt pressing against me. My hand tightens on my glass as I force the mental pictures from my brain.

Looking at her with interest is wrong. Touching her is wrong. Kissing her, moving inside of her … All wrong. But if it was really wrong, why can't I stop thinking about it? If it's really wrong, why do I want her so badly? Why can't I resist her? I'm not the kind of man who has a problem with the word *no*. I've never wanted for what I couldn't have. I've always been responsible, respectable, and honorable. Did that somehow change about me?

If I'd never moved to Chicago, I never would have met her, and I'd be living in New York right now like nothing changed. I'd still be working. I'd still be dating. I wouldn't have all these questions about myself. I'd know without a doubt in my mind that I'm still the person I've always been. But I did move to Chicago. I did meet her. And I fell hard. Part of me feels like I should have been turned off the minute I found out who she really is, but that didn't happen, and I don't know why. Finding out who she is didn't make me want her more, but it didn't make me want her less either.

There's something about her that speaks to me. It pulls me in. I'm blinded by her. The night we met, she left a mark on my soul. Somehow, she became a part of me, and my life will never be the same. I will continue to try and keep her at arm's length, but something tells me it's only a matter of time before she catches me in a weak moment. Even the strongest man on earth can only fight for so long. Eventually, everyone falls. The question for me is: How long can I fight?

* * *

I spent the weekend at home, working remotely on the magazine while avoiding going out in fear of running into her. Deep down, I wanted to return to that club where we met. In fact, I even showered and got dressed to go, but then my strength came back just as I was about to walk out the door. With one hand on the knob and one foot outside, I forced myself to turn around. I was torn. Part of me was proud for being strong. The other part was pissed because the monster inside of me didn't get what he wanted. He was hungry, and only she will feed the need. I managed to starve that monster for another day, but that monster will only get hungrier and hungrier with each passing day.

I self-medicated with scotch and whiskey, only sobering up with sleep throughout the night. The alcohol kept the dreams of her away until there was nothing left in my system. When those dreams woke me in the early morning hours, I would get out of bed and start my day as a way of keeping my mind busy. But all weekends have to come to an end. Monday morning rolls around, and I have no choice but to go to the university, where I know I'll be face-to-face with her again.

I'm grabbing a coffee from the cart outside my building when a round of giggles steals my attention. I turn and look at the large group hanging out beneath the big oak tree. Several football players and cheerleaders are gathering there, Kay being one of them. Only she isn't bouncing around or giggling like the other girls. Instead, she's sitting in the grass, using the trunk of the tree as a backrest. Her long legs are out in front of her, crossed at the ankles. My eyes follow her legs upward, moving over her stomach, over her chest, up to her face. Her plump lips are parted and sparkling. Her green eyes are trained on mine. They're framed in long, black lashes, but I can see the intensity in her stare. Her long black hair isn't straight today. It's curled, holding soft curls that frame her gorgeous face. Her eyes suck the air from my lungs, leaving me breathless.

I step up in line and place my order. I hand the man some cash and glance her way while waiting for my coffee. She hasn't moved, but her eyes are only burning hotter the longer they stay on me. I get handed my cup, and I drop the change into the tip jar before turning and starting my walk to the newsroom.

The moment I enter the room, I'm bombarded with students asking me to read their piece and give them suggestions. As I make my way toward my desk in the corner of the room, I get handed paper after paper. I take them all, more than happy to keep my mind busy. Having a seat, I pull out my red pen and get to work. The task at hand is more than enough to keep me busy. I actually zone out and forget about the room, the students, and her. It isn't until I finish the last paper that I look up and see her behind her desk.

I take a deep breath as I stand with the papers in my hand. I move around the room, handing back the papers to their rightful owners.

"Theo?"

Her voice makes me stop. My back goes ramrod straight, and my shoulders square. I take a cleaning breath before turning to face her.

She looks up at me with those big, green eyes of hers—eyes that I know can see straight to my soul. "Everyone said you read their pieces and gave them some feedback. Would you mind doing that for me?" She holds the paper up between us.

I look from her eyes to the paper and back. "Yeah, sure." I take it, and she offers a smile as she falls back a step.

"Thank you."

I nod as I push myself forward, back to my desk. My heart is racing just from being close to her. I'm breathless from looking into her eyes. I'm glad I'm sitting down now because I'm slightly dizzy, and I wouldn't be surprised if I fell over. I don't know how she sucks the air from the room like she does, but I wonder if anyone else notices it as much as I do.

I grab my red pen and train my eyes on the paper that she's neatly typed out. This is her interview piece on a few of the members who are putting together the first play of the year, and while I find that she's asked good and deep questions, I don't like the way she's formatted the article, and I don't like how her opinion has slipped into her writing when talking about the play. I leave some notes on the paper, just a few suggestions on how I would like to see them.

While reading over her paper, a few other students brought their articles up for me to review as well. When I finish with Kay's, I set it aside and continue with the next in line. I read the three other students' papers, noticing how the room is starting to empty. But Kay still looks to be hard at work, and I can't help but to wonder if she's waiting to talk to me about her paper. I don't know if I can handle that today. I plan on giving these papers back and then leaving campus. I need to put some distance between us.

I pass out the papers and go back to my desk to clean up. I put the cap back on my pen and toss it into the cup on the corner. I grab my empty coffee cup and drop it into the trash. Then I slide my phone back into my pocket and push up my chair. Just as I'm turning to leave, I come to a sudden stop to keep myself from walking into her.

My eyes fall down to hers, my brows pulling together in confusion. "Is there something I can do for you?" I ask, quickly glancing around the room, hoping and praying that other students are present. Unfortunately, everyone else has already left. We're alone. Just her and me. My heart leaps to life, and every muscle tightens to keep myself in check.

"Your comment here." She points at my writing on her paper. "You don't like the way I formatted the article?" Her big green eyes lock on mine, her perfectly trimmed brow arches.

I nod, squaring my shoulders. "That's right. It's a little too Q&A, like it's from a grade school paper. I'd like to see the interview written out with quotes."

She puts her hand on her hip. "Well, this is the way that the editor wants interviews published in the paper. Is this something the two of you have talked about because I have better things to do than to rewrite this article only to find out that the original was right all along."

I cross my arms over my chest. "I haven't discussed this with the editor, but my job here is to bring this paper back from the dead. This is one of the changes I'd suggest be made. If he gives you any problems, just send him to me. I promise, it won't be a waste writing it a second time." I go to step past her, but I pause when she says …

"Also …" She frowns up at me. "Since when is it bad for my opinion to be in the article I'm writing? It shows that this article was written by a person with thoughts and ideas. Not some robot who is objective with no feelings."

"This isn't an editorial. Your opinions are not needed for this interview. You should remain biased. Let the readers make up their minds for themselves. This article reads like you're trying to convince them to skip the play."

"I am trying to convince them to skip the play. This is a horribly outdated play that should have been removed from schools everywhere years ago."

I shake my head. "Your assignment was not to give your opinion. It was to interview those involved with the play. Sure, you did half your job by giving the interview. But nobody asked for your input on the topic of the play. The next time the paper needs an opinion-based article, I'll be sure to come to you. As for now, rewrite it." I step past her, heading for the door.

"Is this really because you hate my article, or is this about something else?"

I turn back to face her. "What else would this be about?"

Her brow arches. "I think these comments don't have anything to do with my writing or this paper." She crosses her arms over her chest as she takes slow steps toward me. "I think you're being harder on me because of the night we spent together."

I hold up my index finger, pointing at her. "Do not ever. Mention that night again. You understand me?"

She frowns.

I step toward her, needing to lower my voice but wanting to make sure she can hear me. She's directly in front of me now, with only a few inches between us. I can feel the heat leaving her body. I can smell the scent of her perfume. Hell, I'm close enough that I can feel her warm breath as it blows against my face as she nervously looks up at me. "The last thing either of us needs is for that little secret to get out. I'm now an employee here at the university. You're a student. You think the dean would care that you *technically* weren't my student the night that happened? Or how about your father? How do you think he'd feel knowing his daughter went home with a perfect stranger she drunkenly met in a crowded club? I'm pretty sure he wouldn't approve. I'm not the only one with something to lose here, Kay. I suggest you forget all about that night and never mention it again." I turn but stop when her voice hits my ears.

"I'll forget about it when you do." Her tone is matter-of-fact.

My eyes level on hers. "What's that supposed to mean?"

She lets out a quiet chuckle as she gently shakes her head. Her back straightens, and her chest puffs out. "You're going to sit here and preach to me about forgetting about that night when you can't forget about it either."

I open my mouth to argue, but she cuts me off.

"Don't try and deny it. I've seen it with my own two eyes. I saw the way you looked at me when I was cheering at the game. I saw the jealousy when Xander picked me up and threw me over his shoulder. I see the way you look at me in class. And I notice when you stand at the coffee cart, just staring off in my general direction as I hang out with my friends. You can't forget about this either."

Without another word, I turn and walk out of the class as quickly, but as steadily, as I can. I can't get space between us fast enough.

My heart is pounding as I push my way out of the building. My hands are itching to feel her soft skin. My whole body is tingling, needing to feel her pressed against me. And my dick … it's begging me to march back in there and bend her over my desk, make her mine once again. It takes every ounce of strength I have to walk away as fast as fucking possible.

KAYLEE

I stand back, surprised when he just turns and walks away from me. I expected him to deny the accusation, but he didn't. Last week, I was sure he hated me with the way he was avoiding me. But that game changed everything. I saw the heat in his eyes, even with a football field between us. He still wants me. He's just afraid to act on it. But I'm not.

I grab my bag and exit the newsroom, heading down the hall for the main doors of the building. Theo was in a hurry to get out, but my dad must have caught up to him because they're standing close to the exit, talking in the hallway. Dad has his back to me as I approach. Theo's facing me, his eyes moving from my dad's face to me as I approach. His jaw flexes, and I notice his chest expand as he takes a deep breath. I don't say anything as I pass, and neither does he. To my surprise, my dad even lets me walk by without trying to get my attention. Outside, I suck in a deep breath of fresh air. It's the first breath I've taken that hasn't had faint notes of his cologne. It's almost like I can get high just from breathing the same air as him. Now, he's no longer in sight, so I'm slowly coming down, and to be honest, I don't like it.

"Kay!"

I turn to see Margo standing with some of the guys by the gym. She smiles and waves me over. I tighten my hand on my bag, hiking it higher up on my shoulder as I make my way to the next building.

She wraps her arm around my neck, pulling me in for a hug. "We were just talking about the Halloween party."

I pat her back before pulling away. "The Halloween party? That's months away."

She nods. "Yeah, but planning starts now. I mean, we have to put together the fundraisers to pay for the party, and then we have to plan all the attractions. You're going to help, right?"

"I..."

Xander puts his arm around my shoulders. "Come on, Kay. This is our senior year. You may as well enjoy it while you can. Halloween is one of the best parties of the year."

Margo nods in agreement. So do the other guys who are currently hanging out. I look at each of them before my eyes catch movement off in the distance. I look up to find Theo walking out of the building I just vacated. His eyes find me immediately. I see the way the fire burns within them, the way his jaw tenses. I realize what this must look like to him. Almost every time he sees me out of class, I have Xander at my side—it's not planned; it just works out that way. He probably thinks I'm just toying with him at this point.

"I'm not sure, guys. I have to go." I step away, causing Xander's arm to fall away as I make my way down the sidewalk.

The group behind me groans at my quick escape, but I pay them no mind as I continue to walk away. I don't go after Theo. I can't since we're in public, but I start my walk home, hoping that Theo watched me walk away from Xander. I want Theo to see me leave Xander behind. I need him to understand that I don't want anything to do with another guy. Maybe if he sees that, he'll be able to let his guard down, and maybe he'll let me in.

I can feel Theo's closeness to me as I walk across campus. It isn't until I pass through the parking lot that I can no longer feel him. Glancing over my shoulder, I see that he's gone. It feels like my heart drops to my stomach as I glance around the parking lot for him. Then I see him as he climbs behind the wheel of his car. A moment later, he's slowly driving past me, and our eyes lock through the window. Neither of us smiles or waves, and he doesn't stop. There's no contact of any kind, but somehow, I can still feel whatever this is between us. I can feel it tugging at something in my chest, in my belly. It causes the butterflies in my stomach to come alive once again as my blood warms.

He pulls out into traffic, and he drives away, leaving me behind. But still, all I can think about is the night we shared together while my body begs for his touch once more. As I walk to my apartment, I can't stop myself from trying to figure out a way to make this work. I know he'll never touch me on campus. It's too dangerous because anyone could walk in on us—anyone being my father. I highly doubt he's planning on going back to that club anytime soon, and I've never bumped into him anywhere else off campus. I don't have his phone number since we never exchanged them. All I do know is where he lives. Should I go to his apartment uninvited?

No, I can't do that. That's rude. In fact, I know I should just let this go like he suggested, but I can't. Being with him was unlike anything I've ever experienced. He was different—everything about him. The way his eyes would darken and burn, it was like he could see right through me. The way he'd touch me, kiss me—every moment of being together was teasing and pleasurable. Just thinking about how his eyes intensified on mine right before he'd lean in and kiss me has my skin breaking out in goosebumps. The emotions he caused me to feel, it's not something I can just walk away from. I have to figure out how to make him forget about how complicated things can be and just get him to focus on how good things can be between us.

I make it home, and I get all of my assignments done. I'm sitting on the couch watching TV when Margo walks in. She drops her bag by the door. Grabbing a soda from the kitchen, she moves to sit on the opposite end of the couch. She pops the top of her soda before looking over at me. "Okay, I have to know what is going on with you this year. This isn't still about Travis, is it?"

I look over at her. "What do you mean?"

She rolls her eyes. "Last year, you went to every single party. You even helped plan them. You were going on a date every weekend, and you were almost never home. Then you break up with Travis, and everything changes. You went home for almost the entire summer. Now, you're not wanting to plan parties or attend them. You're not dating. I mean, Xander has asked you out how many times now? You're always here. You need to get out and have a life."

I want to roll my eyes. "I'm just …" How do I explain? "I'm just tired of the college life. I'm sick of my life revolving around parties and dates. No, this isn't about Travis or our breakup. I'm just over it. It feels like my college life is just a repeat of my high school life, and I'm done. I want to get my degree so I can move out and get on with my life. I want to focus on my career instead of getting drunk at some party. Is that really that bad?"

She sips her soda. "Kay, this is the last year you get to be a carefree college kid. Next year, you're an adult, and you'll spend the rest of your life that way. You need to enjoy every minute you can."

I offer a sad smile. "I am. It's just that what I enjoy … it's no longer parties and football players." I shrug one shoulder.

She scoffs. "Yeah, I guess I can understand that. We should do something just the two of us, no boys allowed."

I smile. "What do you suggest?"

She thinks for a moment before her eyes stretch wide, and she smiles. "Movie night. We can order pizza and stuff ourselves with junk food until we're in a coma from the sugar crash. What do you say?"

It's not like I have a better way of spending my evening, so I nod. "It's a date," I agree.

"Okay, give me one hour to get my homework done, and then we'll order some dinner and pick a movie." She jumps off the couch. Grabbing her bag and soda, she runs to her room to get to work.

While I wait, I decide to take an early shower so that I can just go right to sleep after our movie. I take my time cleaning up, and when I get out, I blow-dry my hair. I don't bother with making it look presentable. Instead, I just pull it into a high, messy ponytail. I also don't bother with getting dressed in day clothes, opting for something a little more comfortable to lounge around in. I pull on a pair of black joggers and the matching cropped sweatshirt. Then I add some oversized, slouchy socks before making my way back to the couch.

I scroll through every steaming service we have for a movie to watch, and I order some pizza, breadsticks, and wings. By the time Margo is done with her homework, I've already picked the movie and gotten the food ordered. For the next two hours, we do nothing but watch TV, stuff ourselves, laugh, squeal, and talk our way through the movie like we're a couple of kids. It's easy to forget everything and just have fun with Margo. That is, until the movie is over and she's heading off to bed. I check the time on my phone to see that it's only going on nine. I still have too much energy to go to sleep, and showing up at Theo's apartment is sounding better and better.

I push the thought from my head, focusing on cleaning up our mess from our movie night. I throw out all the boxes and wipe down the coffee table before folding up all the blankets. Turning off the TV and the lamp, I make my way toward my room. I lay down and cuddle up with my pillows and blankets, trying to force myself to sleep, despite the nervous energy racing through my body. The moment my eyes close, my imagination takes me away. I can't stop myself from thinking about how the night could go if I were to show up uninvited. Would he let me in? Would he tell me to leave?

I smile because even though I don't know for sure, I have a pretty good idea. He'd let me in. I know he wants me from the look in his eyes. He's been able to keep me at arm's length, but that's only because we've been in public. I have a feeling he'd have a much harder time resisting me if we were in the privacy of his apartment. Apparently, my imagination has a mind of its own because I don't remember making the decision to fantasize about him, about the things we'd do if I did show up at his apartment tonight, but I find myself imagining kissing him again. I can practically feel the warmth of his lips against mine. The smell of his cologne washes over me, and I breathe it in deeply, to the point where my nose actually burns. My blood warms, and my heart starts to race. Every nerve ending tingles, sending a wave throughout my entire body that pushes me to do something I said I wouldn't.

I throw back the blanket and climb out of bed. I slide my feet into some slides before grabbing my keys and phone. Then, I slip out of the apartment undetected to make the drive over to his apartment. I'm filled with nervous energy as I walk down the hallway that leads to his door. What was I thinking? Of course, he's going to turn me away. We may not have been breaking any rules the first time, but now we will be. And I'm making a conscious decision to do so. Does that stop me?

No.

I'm too far gone.

I'm too close to turn back now.

I raise my fist and knock against his door, the sound echoing around the empty hallway.

The door gets pulled open quickly, and I feel like all the noise is only drawing attention to me. That feeling causes me to fall back a step, but then our eyes lock, and nothing else matters.

THEO

Maybe I've had too much to drink tonight. Maybe this moment isn't even real. Maybe I passed out, and I'm dreaming. That isn't so hard to believe after all. How many nights have I fallen asleep, only to dream of her coming over like this? This is probably the hundredth time I've had this exact dream. Except, usually she doesn't show up in sweats and a messy ponytail. Usually ... it's a trench coat that she opens to reveal nothing under it. Or she's only wearing black lace panties, a matching bra, and a garter belt with killer heels. In my dreams, the moment our eyes lock, she's throwing herself into my arms as our mouths crash together. That's when I pick her up against me and carry her inside. Only ... she isn't throwing herself into my arms. She's looking at me like a deer in the headlights. That's when I put it all together to realize that this isn't a dream. She's really here, standing in front of my open door, where anyone can see.

"What the hell are you doing here?" I ask, glancing around the hallway to make sure nobody is witnessing this.

She runs that sweet tongue of hers across those soft lips, making them glisten under the lights. "Can we talk?"

"This is highly inappropriate. What if someone saw you coming up here?"

Her brows lift. "The longer you make me stand here, the bigger that chance gets."

A heavy sigh leaves my lips as I fall back a step, opening the door wider for her.

She walks in, and I'm quick to shut the door before turning to face her. She's already walking over to the floor-to-ceiling windows to look out at the city lights—just like she did the first time I brought her here. I can't stop myself from watching her. Even dressed down, she's breathtaking. Her black joggers are fitted, hugging her rounded ass. I get an instant flash of what that ass looked like—the way it rippled when I thrust into her from behind. I shake my head, my hand moving up to rub my eyes.

"What are you doing here, Kay?" My hand falls away as I lift my head to look at her.

She turns to face me, arms crossed over her chest, which only causes her cropped sweatshirt to reveal more of her toned stomach. "I didn't like the way we left things today."

"So you thought you needed to show up, uninvited, to my apartment at ten o'clock at night to discuss it?"

"It's not like we can have this conversation on campus. Someone could overhear, and I never see you anywhere off campus. What choice did I have?"

"There isn't a choice. Don't you see that? You're my student. I'm friends with your father. I mean ... what is it that you want from me?"

"I want you to admit that you enjoyed the night we spent together just as much as I did."

"You know I did." The words are barely above a whisper.

"Okay. If you enjoyed it, and I enjoyed it, then why are we fighting it?"

"We had one night, Kay. One." I hold up my index finger. "It's over. Now we know the connections we share, and we know it's wrong. The only thing we can do is forget it happened and move on."

"I can't forget it happened." She steps toward me. "And I know you can't either."

I feel my brows lift at the threat of her challenging me. "I'm trying to. And you're not making it easy." I turn and walk toward the drink cart in the corner of the room. "The way you look at me in class, at that game ..." I shake my head, grabbing a bottle of whiskey and pouring more than enough into a glass. I take a quick sip.

"I see the way you look at me too, you know?"

I turn around to find that she's taken another step toward me.

"I looked into your eyes, and I could see the fire burning within them, even with a huge football field between us. The way you look at me on campus, it makes my stomach tighten. It makes my heart race. It makes my skin tingle and beg for your touch." She takes another step, keeping her blazing green eyes trained on mine.

"I know you think this is wrong. Yes, you're technically my professor this year. But next year, you'll be gone from here, and so will I." She takes another step toward me, and my back straightens. She's getting too close, and I can feel the monster inside of me starting to wake.

"I don't care if you know my dad. I'm a grown woman. I don't need his permission to date. I don't need him to approve of the men I'm with." She's standing directly in front of me now. She doesn't pull her eyes from mine as she takes the glass from my hand. Moving it to her lips, she tips it back, taking a quick sip before setting it on the cart that's just behind me. Her hand moves up to my neck, her fingers lacing into my hair. "I know what I want, Theo, and it's not some football player. It's you." She presses her chest against mine as she lifts up onto her tiptoes. "Don't make me beg, Theo," she whispers, her hot breath blowing across my lips. "Just give in." She softly kisses the corner of my mouth. "Take what we both know you want."

And that's when I break.

My fast movements are rough, but she doesn't seem to mind when I jerk her toward me. My mouth crashes against hers, and our tongues are quick to find one another. She moans into my mouth as I wrap her up in my arms, squeezing her to remind myself that this is real. Every second, every movement is in one fluid-like motion. One second, she's standing in front of me. The next, I'm picking her up against me, and I'm pressing her back to the floor-to-ceiling windows. Her legs are wrapped around my hips, and she's clinging to me like I'm the air she needs to breathe.

God … kissing her feels good. Everything about this moment is better than I ever could have dreamed. It's better than the first time. Right now, I'm in heaven, and when a monster finds heaven, there's nothing you can do to stop him from destroying it.

My hands work their way up her sides, pushing her sweatshirt up as they go. I'm surprised when I feel the bottoms of her bare breasts just beneath them. My thumbs move from the outside of her breast toward the inside. Then my hands cup them and massage them as my mind burns the weight of them into my brain. I pinch her nipples between my thumbs and the side of my hand, making them harden. She gasps and then lets out a soft whimper that makes my dick twitch in my sweatpants.

Tasting her, hearing her, feeling her, have me out of my head. I can't think straight. I can't remember why this is wrong because, right now, it feels so fucking right. All I can think about is getting back inside her perfect little pussy that feels like it was made just for me. Fuck … just thinking about how warm and tight she is when she's wrapped around me makes my balls draw up.

I'm not usually in a hurry. I like to take my time in moments like these, but right now, it's all I can do to stop myself from fucking her against this window. I can't stop myself from treating her sinful body like it was made for my enjoyment, but I don't worry about it because I know she'll enjoy it just as much. That's how perfect we are together. She'll allow me to use her because, in one way or another, she's using me too. We're using one another to get the most powerful high that we've ever experienced. Something we can only feel when we're together.

I pull her sweatshirt up and over her head, tossing it over my shoulder as I bring my mouth back to hers. My hands are on her thighs now, and I force them to release my hips as I set her back on her feet. My lips move from hers, to her chin, up her jaw, and down her neck. I kiss over her collarbone and over the swell of her breast. My hands move up to cup them while my mouth sucks her nipple into my mouth. I swirl my tongue around it and flick it over and over again. She fists my hair, pulling me closer as soft moans and whimpers leave her lips in a rush.

I fall to my knees as I kiss down her stomach. When her pants cut me off, I lean back and look up her body. Her lips are swollen and glistening from our kiss. Her green eyes are hooded with lust and need, her chest rising and falling quickly. I don't look away as I pick up her foot. Her sandal falls onto the floor, and I tug her sock off her foot. Putting her foot on the floor, I look down to do the same with the other, revealing her black painted toenails.

Her bare back is against the glass, her arms down at her sides, with her palms against the window, fingers splayed. We both watch one another as I dip my fingers into the waistband of her pants. She doesn't stop me when I begin pushing them down, over her hips. When her soft, hairless center is exposed to me, it feels like I could die a happy man.

She's not wearing any panties, and I never realized, until right now, how much I love the feeling of her being ready for me.

She steps out of her pants, and I toss them aside. I lean in, burying my face between her legs as I breathe her in. Doing so makes her melt, and she moans. "I don't want you to ever wear panties again." My eyes move up to lock on hers.

She looks down at me, but I can see the questions in her eyes.

"I can't be walking around campus, wondering if you're wearing panties or not. From now on, when I see you, I want to know that you're completely bare under your clothing. That you'll be ready for me to fuck you any time I see fit. Understand?"

Her eyes only burn hotter, and her face flushes. Her nipples harden as she nods.

I lean back in, my tongue licking her lip. I grab her leg, her shin pressing against my palm as I press her knee toward her chest. Putting her foot on my shoulder, she's fully exposed to me. I run my tongue between her folds, and I suck her clit into my mouth. She moans loudly, and then her head falls back against the glass. I lick and suck and tease, making her legs shake and grow weak, but I don't let her come. I want her on the edge for so fucking long; all I have to do is slide into her to have her crashing.

Leaning back, I remove her foot from my shoulder, putting it back on the floor. Her eyes open and lock on mine. "Turn around."

She doesn't question me. She turns around, pressing her chest to the glass. "Look down at the street." I kiss the back of her thigh. "Look at the other buildings." I kiss her asscheek as my hand moves up her inner thigh. I sink two fingers into her, and she gasps. "Do you think they can see us?" I thrust my fingers into her again, biting her firm ass that's right in front of my face. "Has anyone ever watched you come before, Kay?" My fingers slide out, covered in her arousal, which I spread up to her clit. "Answer me. Have you ever been watched?"

"No," she breathes out.

My slick fingers rub against her clit again and again. "Does the idea of hundreds of people watching as I make you beg to come make you excited?" I dip my fingers back into her, gathering more of her excitement to spread between her folds. "I think it does." I stand up behind her, and I push my sweatpants over my hips until my painfully hard dick springs free. I bite her shoulder as I rub my length between her legs. "How bad do you want me to fuck you right now?" I whisper in her ear, my hips moving forward and back to slide my cock against her. She's so excited, her arousal is coating me.

"Please, Theo," she begs with pain in her voice. "I need you so bad."

I run the tip of my nose along her ear. "And what if I told you no? What if I made you get dressed and leave right now? What would you do?"

Her hand moves between her legs, rubbing her clit. I react as quickly as I can. I grab her wrist and pull her hand away, putting it back in place on the window. Her glistening fingers leave a trail on the glass that I consider leaving there forever as a constant reminder of how fast she makes me lose my shit.

"You really think I'd let you touch yourself?" I grind against her entrance, and she whimpers and rocks against me, causing my tip to slide inside. She cries out, and I'm a goner. I can't resist anymore. I thrust deep into her while my arm moves around her hip, my fingers between her legs as I grind into her from behind. That's all it takes to push her over the edge. The second I'm inside her, her muscles are convulsing all around me. My fingers and hips keep their pace, making sure I push her over her limit. The next thing I know, I hear the sounds of something wet splashing into the floor, and liquid is running down both our legs and feet. Making her squirt pulls me over the edge with her.

I don't want to come this early, but it's too fucking perfect to resist. This won't be the end. I'll touch and taste and tease her until we're both begging for it again. And then I'll spend the rest of my night buried in her greedy, responsive little pussy. Right now, my hips take on a life of their own, thrusting into her again and again and allowing us both to ride every last wave of our orgasm. Neither of us can get enough until we have nothing left to lose.

KAYLEE

My release is so strong that it leaves me feeling weak. When he pulls out of me, I can't even stand on my own. My feet are numb and tingling, and my legs feel like Jello. Luckily, he catches me in his strong arms. Picking me up against him, he carries me to his bathroom, and he walks us into the shower. He turns the water on, and we're blasted with cold water. I jerk in his arms, but he holds tight. Seconds later, the water is warm and welcoming, and I relax against him.

He presses my back to the tiled wall, and he moves his mouth to mine. He kisses me softly and slowly. He's never kissed me like this before. I love the way he's kissed me in the past. I like it when he's rough and forceful with me, because that tells me he's just as passionate as I am. Now I'm learning that maybe I like it this way too—soft and slow—something I've never enjoyed with anyone before him.

He forces me to loosen my legs around him, and when I do, my feet fall onto the floor. He doesn't break our kiss, but he spins me so the water is raining over my hair. His hands move up to work the water into my locks. When it's fully soaked, I hear an automatic dispenser. Seconds later, he's working my hair into a lather.

I've never had a man take care of me in this way. Sure, I've had boyfriends in high school and a few in my early years of college, but I never got this intimate with them. Travis is the guy I dated the longest, and even though we'd showered together a couple of times, it was mostly him freezing in the back while I cleaned myself. I've never had a man worry about cleaning me before. I can't help but relax into him.

He breaks our kiss. "Lean your head back."

I do, and he starts rinsing the shampoo from my hair. With his hands busy in my hair, he moves his lips back to my jaw, kissing his way down my neck and bringing my body back to life. Every way he touches me, teases me—even when those touches are nothing but innocent. When he finishes with my hair, he fills his hands with body wash, and then he takes his time working the soap into a lather across my skin. He washes my hands, arms, and shoulders. His hands glide up my neck, and a fire lights in my belly when I feel his hands around my throat. They slide down over my breasts. He even washes under them before spreading the soap over my ribs, sides, and stomach. Then he washes my hips and between my legs. Again, he isn't trying to pleasure me, yet having him touch me and care for me is teasing. When he's finished working the soap over my skin, he grabs the shower head and starts to rinse the bubbles down my body.

The hard spray from the handheld shower head makes my nipples harden. He watches them, his jaw flexing and his eyes darkening. He moves the shower head lower, rinsing off my stomach, my hips, and then he directs it to spray between my legs. I jump, my hand moving to his to redirect the spray, only he doesn't let me.

His eyes move back up to mine, and I see the challenge in them. My hand falls from his as I press myself against the shower wall. I watch the way his eyes move down my body, down between my legs, to watch the water tease my clit. His Adam's apple bobs, and his jaw flexes. His chest starts to rise and fall, and I watch as he grows harder and harder. I would normally have no interest in the shower head. I never would've let Travis do something like this, but I like pushing my boundaries with him. I like to see the way his dirty mind works, and I like watching him respond to the way I respond to him.

I know he won't let me take the shower head, so I wrap my hand around his cock instead. His eyes bounce back to mine as I slowly start working him up and down. I bite my lower lip, watching as his eyes start to roll to the back of his head. When I know he's weak, I drop down to my knees before him. I look up his body, and our eyes connect, but he doesn't stop me as I guide his tip between my lips. I suck him into my mouth, working him deeper and deeper to the back of my throat. I don't worry about being messy since we're both already in the shower. I take him deeper, and I move faster and faster. I gag several times, which he seems to enjoy—something about the way my esophagus tenses around his length. I have slobber dripping from my mouth, stringing down and dripping onto the shower floor.

His breathing gets harder and harder before he moans and mutters a weak, "Fuck, Kay. Mmmmmm, you have to stop, beautiful."

I don't want to stop. I want to make him feel just as weak as he makes me feel.

"I want to spend the rest of the night buried deep inside that greedy little pussy of yours, and I won't be able to do that if you make me come again, angel." His head falls back. "Fuuuck. How do you do this so good?"

I want to smile, but my mouth is full. On the inside, though, I'm smiling, laughing, cheering, dancing.

"Stop right now, Kay. If you want me back between your legs tonight, stop right now." His breathing is getting louder, and I can tell he's on the brink of his release. Still, I can't ignore his threat, as much as I want to. I release him, and the second I do, he's fisting my hair and pulling me to my feet. His mouth catches mine, and he gathers me in his arms once again.

He shuts off the shower, and he picks me up, carrying me to his bedroom, even though we're both soaking wet. We go tumbling into the bed, the blankets and sheets sticking to our wet skin, but that doesn't stop him from getting where he wants to be: between my legs. His mouth and his hands seem to touch and kiss every inch of my body. He licks, bites, sucks. His hands squeeze, tease, and caress. He's not just pleasuring me; he's worshipping my body. I'm nearly ready to come undone when he rocks into me, making us one. He doesn't hold back or go slow. He slides in until there's nothing left to give. I'm suddenly too full. Pain rips through me from the way I'm stretching around him, but once he's in position, his hips are still, letting me adjust.

He's on his knees, and he has my lower body angled in an upward motion. His hands are on my hips, and he's holding me still as he rolls his hips into me again and again. My fists are wrapped around the iron bars of his headboard as I moan and cry out his name for more.

"That's right, angel. Take every inch." His right hand moves between my legs for only a second. Before I know what's happening, his hand is under my ass, his thumb sliding between my cheeks.

I've never felt so full before. I've never felt so excited and content all at the same time. It's like every emotion is being felt at once. I'm so overwhelmed that, when my orgasm crashes over me, I think I black out. It takes me like a wave, picking my body up and bashing me against the rocks again, and again, and again. I can't breathe. I can't think. I'm hostage to my orgasm until I'm released and my ride ends. When I snap out of my daze, we're both soaked and dripping with my excitement. He's grunting and growling as he drives into me, finishing out his release.

We're both too weak to try and clean the bed. He collapses at my side, both our breathing ragged as he gathers me in his arms. The blanket was kicked to the foot of the bed, so he pulls it back up and over us. Then he holds me tight against his chest until I'm fast asleep.

* * *

I wake up early in the morning. I roll from my side to my back, finding the other side of the bed empty. I lift my head, looking at the open bathroom door. The light is off, so I know he's not inside. I crawl out of bed and use the restroom. In the bedroom, I open the dresser and pull out one of his t-shirts, and I pull it on before I venture into the rest of his apartment. Walking into the living room, I find him sitting on the couch, wearing nothing but his boxers.

The room is only lit up by the dark sky outside. The sun is coming up, but it isn't up yet, so the room is a soft shade of blue. I move over to the couch, sitting at his side. He takes a sip of his coffee, and I nearly jump when he speaks.

"Last night was a mistake." His jaw flexes, and his Adam's apple bobs. "I need you to get dressed and leave. Never come here again. Understand?"

He isn't looking at me. "Theo," I breathe out.

"No, this never should have happened. Last night was …" His jaw twitches. "Last night was one of the best nights of my life. I've never been so raw with anyone before, but—"

I take the cup of coffee from his hands, causing the words to fall from his lips. His eyes move over to mine, watching as I take a sip of the bitter, lukewarm coffee. I lean forward and set the cup on the coffee table. Then I swing my knee over him until I'm settled on his lap. His eyes burn, but he's trying so damn hard to be good. He's holding his hands up in the air, like I've told him to freeze.

"I'm not going anywhere, Theo." I lean in, kissing the corner of his mouth. "I will not walk out of that door so you can forget last night happened." I lace my fingers into the back of his hair, and I yank his head back until he has no choice but to meet my gaze. "You and me, this …" I motion between us with my free hand. "It's so hard to resist because we're not supposed to resist it. Can't you see that I'm your weakness and you're mine? This isn't bad or wrong in the grand scheme of things. This is perfect." I feel him growing hard beneath me, so I reach between us and free him from his boxers. Wrapping my hand around him, I start to slowly pump from base to tip. "The reason it feels so good when we touch … It's nature's way of telling us that we found what everyone is looking for. I'm your other half. Stop resisting it. Stop fighting it and just give in." With him hard in my hand, I lift my hips and place him at my entrance.

I almost expect him to try and push me away, but he doesn't even fight it. His hands find my hips, and the moment I have him in place, he's pulling me down so his cock is parting my walls as he slides into me.

"Mmmmm," he mutters, his hands tightening on my hips. "You're right."

My heart leaps to life with those words. It feels like it lodges itself in my throat.

"You are mine now, Kaylee." He leans in, kissing me. "You're the dark angel sent from hell to trap me." He rocks me against him. "You're here to take me to hell for my sins. I bet the devil didn't think I'd fall for my captor." He lifts me up and pulls me back down his length. "Take this off." He pinches my shirt, so I quickly do as he says, leaving me completely naked as I ride him on the couch in his living room.

"So much fucking better." He grins, his eyes fully taking me in. "I always want to see every inch of you, angel. Fuck, I love watching this beautiful pussy stretching around my dick. Lean back for me, beautiful."

I move my hand to his knees that are behind me, and I lean back as far as I can without falling.

"Fuck, Kaylee … I want to come just from watching you ride me. Tell me how good I feel moving inside of you."

"So good," I breathe out, letting him lift me up and pull me back down faster and faster. Already, my release is building.

"That's right, baby. You know I'm the only one who can make you feel like this, don't you?"

A moan slips from my lips as I nod.

"I'm the only one who can make you scream for more while you're begging me to stop." He is thrusting into me now, and they're getting harder and faster. "I'm the only one who can make you come harder than you've ever come before, aren't I?" He buries himself deeper, and I scream when my orgasm hits me. It rolls through my body in waves that get more and more intense. "Yes, Kay. Come for me, baby. Fuck, you're so fucking wet for me." His hips jerk, and he grunts. I feel his warm release spill into me, like lotion to a sunburn, as we both slow to a stop.

I collapse against his chest, and he holds me against him while we both take a moment to even our breathing. After we've collected ourselves, he holds me tight, and he stands up, moving us back toward the bedroom. He lays me on the bed and climbs up behind me. He pulls the blankets up over us, and he wraps me in his arms. He brushes my hair away from my face, and he breathes me in deeply.

"You know we've fucked up, right?"

I glance at him from over my shoulder.

"I tried to do the right thing. I tried to chase you off. I tried to set you free. But you wouldn't go." He shakes his head. "Now you're mine, and when something is mine, I don't let it go."

I roll over so I'm facing him, and he moves his hand to cup my cheek. "These eyes are mine. These lips are mine …" He leans in, kissing me.

And before I know it, we're wrapped up in one another all over again.

THEO

We both wake up when my alarm goes off at 7 a.m. I quickly silence it, and as I'm rolling back over to her, I realize she's already crawling out of bed. I leap toward her, trying to wrap my arms around her waist. "What are you doing?" I ask when I miss.

She giggles as she comes to a stop by the door. "I have to get my clothes on and get home. If I time this right, I can be sneaking in the door while Margo is in the shower. Then I won't have to explain why I'm walking into our apartment, where she thinks I've been all night." She slips out the door, but she's back a second later, holding her clothes to her chest.

"I heard someone in the kitchen," she whispers.

I wave my hand through the air as I watch her shake her hips from side to side to get her pants in place. "It's just my assistant. He won't say a word about anything he sees."

She rolls her eyes as she pulls her sweatshirt on. "You could've warned me. What if he walked out of the kitchen and saw me naked?"

I chuckle. "I'm sorry. I wasn't thinking about him. I was too busy watching that ass of yours shake as you made your way to the door."

She softens as she sits on the bed to pull on her socks. Now, she's within reach. I wrap my arms around her and pull her back to me. I pin her beneath me, and I kiss her neck and jaw. "We still have a lot of stuff to talk about."

"I know because we didn't do much talking at all last night … Or this morning."

I pull back to see her breathtaking smile. "You were right. I don't want to let this go, but I'm not sure how it can work."

She cups my jaw. "We just have to be careful. At school, you're just my professor and my dad's friend. But when we're here and there's no other eyes on us, we're free to be together however we want." She lifts her head, planting a kiss to my mouth.

"And when we're out there …" I nod toward the outside world. "Are you considering yourself single or taken?"

"I only belong to you, Theo. Even if the rest of the world doesn't know it."

I can't help the smile that tugs at my lips.

"But, just so you know … you belong to me too now."

I chuckle and nod. "I think I can handle that," I agree, moving back in to kiss her. Using my hips, I part her legs and slide down between them. "Now, about this overly eager football player …"

She laughs. "You have nothing to worry about. I've been turning Xander down every time he approaches me. He'll get the hint one of these days."

I know this is something we're just going to have to figure out. I'm going to have to control my jealousy, especially when I see him chasing after her. I want the whole world to know that she's mine, but that can't happen. It's not that she can tell him she's seeing someone else to get him to back off. If she does that, he'll wonder who it is, word will spread, and everyone will be watching her to figure out who it is. That's something else we don't need. We need to hide in the shadows. It's the only chance we have at making this work.

I have no choice but to release her. I pull on my sweatpants, and I show her to the door, where I give her another goodbye kiss. Once she's finally slipped away, I turn with a smile and head for the shower.

The smile just won't leave my lips today. I'm happy—unbelievably so. I got the girl who's been tormenting my dreams. Even if we do have to keep things quiet, I know that she'll always be trying to make her way back to me. I'm actually looking forward to seeing her on campus now, which only makes me want to get out the door that much faster.

I shower, get ready, and have some breakfast and coffee before making the drive to campus. Of course, she's hanging out with her usual group as I'm stopping to get a cup of coffee from the cart. Our eyes lock, and a knowing smile tugs at her lips. Her green eyes sparkle, and my dick twitches because I know exactly what she's thinking about with that sparkle in her eye: last night, this morning, all the ways I touched and kissed her, how many times I made her shatter.

She pulls her eyes from mine, and her cheeks turn pink as she bites down on her bottom lip. I get my coffee, and I start the walk to class, glancing toward her every few steps until I'm walking into the building. I shake my head at myself. You'd think I was some giddy fifteen-year-old boy again. I can't help it, though. There's just something about her that makes me want to smile. I want to throw her over my shoulder and run away with her, keeping her all to myself. Maybe we can get on my yacht and spend a few months just cruising around the ocean. I want to be able to touch her any time I want. I want her to be all mine. I don't want to share her with the world.

"Theo."

I stop my walk to class, turning around when I hear my name. I look up to see Asher walking over to me.

"Hey, what's going on?" I ask, shaking his hand.

He smiles and shakes his head. "Nothing. What's going on with you?"

I shrug. "Nothing. Why, you ask?"

He looks me up and down as his smile only grows bigger. "I just … I haven't seen you look this happy in … I don't know how long. Everything okay?"

I wipe the smile from my lips—I wasn't even aware that it was still in place. "Oh, everything's fine. Just woke up on the right side of the bed this morning. That's all." And any side of the bed is the right side when his daughter is on the other end. Fuck … I want to punch myself. I can't be thinking about shit like this when he's standing in front of me. I know he can't read my mind, but I want to avoid any and all questions if at all possible.

He nods. "Okay, well, I just wanted to stop you to see if you had plans for this weekend. Meredith and I thought it would be nice to invite you to this little place we know for brunch. Then you and I can spend the rest of the day fishing while she goes off and does … whatever she does."

"Oh, well, thanks for the invite, but I do have plans. I'm going back to New York for this event I RSVP'd two months ago. But enjoy the weekend. It sounds like you have a fun day planned." I pat his shoulder before turning and making my way to class.

* * *

I check the time on my watch, and my eyes move up to take in the students who are still in the newsroom. My eyes automatically meet Kay's. She offers me a smile, and she bats her lashes before she moves her pen to her mouth. She goes back to looking at the computer screen, but I watch as she drags the end of her pen across her bottom lip and back. I remember the way it felt when she did that with my dick, and a bolt of lightning strikes within my system. Her mouth opens, and she slides the end of her pen between her lips. Her mouth closes around her pen, and she slowly moves the pen in and out—only slightly so nobody would notice. But I notice. Not only do I notice, it turns me on, and she knows it.

I clear my throat and pull my eyes away. A few people in class glance my way, but most of them go back to what they're working on. A couple of them leave, and that's when I notice her watching me again. I can feel the keys in my pocket, and an idea hits me. It's not a good idea. In fact, it's a very bad idea, but it's an idea I can't resist.

When she looks at me again, I move my eyes toward the door, and then I get up and make my way out. I slowly walk down the hallway and then out of the building. She's busy looking at her phone screen as she follows behind me, but she's far enough back that nobody would ever guess we were going to the same place. She keeps her attention on her screen, but I know it's only a prop.

I walk into the library, and then I make my way through the rows and rows of books until I come to the archives. I put the key into the lock and step inside, waiting for her to find me. I was given the only key to this room so I could go back and look at past issues of the paper. I never intended on using it for this.

I hear her quiet footsteps, and I open the door, causing her to jump. I smile, grab her hand, and pull her in.

"What are you doing?" she whispers, already cupping my jaw for a kiss.

"You know what I'm doing," I tell her, pressing her back against the door. "I wanted to see if you were following orders." I teasingly bite her lower lip.

"Following orders?" she asks, looking up at me.

"Drop them."

She rolls her eyes, but she walks around me so she's standing in the center of the room. Her hands move to the button on her jeans. Slowly, she pushes them down her hips, showing me that she does know how to follow orders because she isn't wearing any panties. I'm instantly hard, and my mouth is watering for a taste. Only, we don't have much time. The faster we can make this, the better.

My hands move to unfasten my belt. "Bend over the table," I tell her, freeing myself from my jeans as I walk toward her.

She turns, so the table is in front of her. Then she bends over nicely and slowly.

I suck two fingers into my mouth, coating them in my spit. Then I move them between her legs, rubbing against her clit to get her warmed up. I watch her wiggle her ass from side to side for me, and her legs begin to shake. That's when I know she's ready for me. Taking myself in hand, I press my tip to her entrance. I swirl myself around her opening, coating my head with her excitement. Once I'm good and lubed up, I thrust forward, making us one.

She stifles a moan when my hip bones slam against her ass. My hands tighten on her hips, and my head falls forward. "Fuck, you feel so good, Kay." I grind against her. "Are you sore, baby? Have you had enough of me?"

"No," she whines quietly. "Fuck me, Theo. Hard and fast. I need you now."

I've never been able to resist her, and I can't do anything but give her exactly what she asks for. I hold her hips in my hands, and I thrust forward and back, fast and hard, over and over and over until she's shattering around me, and I'm emptying myself into her.

I pull myself out, even though we're both still breathless. I notice the way my load wants to follow the same path, but I like the idea of her walking around campus with my come dripping from her perfect pussy ... Especially if that football player comes sniffing around her again.

I place my hand in the center of her back, and I hold her against the table. Two fingers from my free hand move between her legs, pushing my load back up inside of her. She has no idea what I'm doing, and I like the idea of claiming her without her even knowing. I pull my fingers back and slide them into her again with a little more force, basically fucking her with my fingers now that my dick is spent. Her ass wiggles in front of me as I hold her in place, pushing her over the edge once again.

I remove my fingers from her, and I smack her playfully on the ass. Bending over, I press a kiss to the red print I left behind. "Good girl."

I help her stand upright, and after tucking myself away, I pull up her jeans and button them.

"So, if I'm good, I get ..."

I smirk. "If you're good, I'll make sure you come again and again and again." I zip her jeans.

"And if I'm bad?"

"If I find that you've worn panties to campus, I'll tease and torture." I grin.

She smiles as she wraps her arms around my neck, pulling me in for a kiss. "Should I come by your place tonight? We can make plans for this weekend."

"I can't." I pull back and move toward the door. "I have plans this weekend, and I'm due back in the city."

That hopeful expression falls from her face, and it pains me. "Oh."

I take her hand, and I pull her closer. Spinning her around, I press her back to the door. "I'm sorry. I've had these engagements for months. But I promise, I'll make it up to you." I kiss the corner of her mouth. "You know I'll be thinking of you the entire time I'm gone, right?" I bite her lower lip.

She grins and nods. "You better make it up to me." She pushes against my chest until I fall back a step. Then she pulls the door open and slips out, leaving me alone with my heart racing only for her. I don't know what it is about her, but she knows how to get to me.

I'm cussing myself now for the commitment I made months ago. At the time, I thought I'd still be in New York. I often went to all kinds of social gatherings and events as a way of getting eyes on the company. I had no idea I'd move to Chicago and fall head over heels for a woman I met in the club. I had no idea I'd be so wrapped up in that woman that I can't think straight. That's never happened to me before. I used to be a serial dater. I've been with many beautiful women over the years. Yet none of them got their claws in me like she did.

The night we met, she changed something inside of me. I'll never be the same again.

KAYLEE

"Girl, you are glowing," Margo says as she stands at my side on the field.

I roll my eyes and feel my face heat up, but I try and ignore her as I jump up and down, excited by a tackle on the field.

"What are you doing differently?"

I scoff. "What? Nothing."

Her eyes narrow on my face, trying to figure out all of my secrets. "Your makeup is the same. Your hair seems extra bouncy, but I haven't seen any new products in the shower." She gasps. "Are you taking products out of the bathroom so I can't use them?" She points her finger at me. "We promised we'd share that kind of stuff, remember? It's not fair that your hair looks so good while mine is all lifeless." She twirls a strand around her finger.

I want to laugh. I didn't realize Theo's shampoo was so much better than mine, but it smells like him, so I loved catching a whiff of it all day. "No, I haven't changed anything. Stop being paranoid."

That shuts her up. She hates it when she's called paranoid. She puts her hands on her hips and turns her attention back to the game. She doesn't talk to me as we cheer for the team. When the game ends and the guys start running over, I turn and hightail it out of there, having no interest whatsoever in going to a party. I slip off the field and blend in with the crowd as I make my way toward my car in the lot.

When I get home, I take off my cheer uniform and pull on some shorts and a tank top. I take my hair out of its ponytail and let it cascade around my face and shoulders. It is extra soft and bouncy from Theo's products. And I love the way his scent surrounds me. It makes goosebumps appear on my skin, almost like he's about to step up behind me and touch me or kiss me.

My phone rings, and I jump from my daydream. I pick it up and put it to my ear. "Hello?"

"Hi, gorgeous," he says on the other end of the line.

I smile when his deep, raspy voice washes over me. "How'd you get my number?"

He chuckles. "I may have broken into your phone last night. Are you mad at me?"

I lay down on my bed, curling up in a ball. "No. I'm glad you did. I was just thinking about you."

"You were?"

"Mmm-hmm."

"How'd the game go?"

"Good, we won." I roll onto my back, looking up at the ceiling.

"No party?"

I snort. "Oh, there's a party, but I'm skipping it. I wish you were home. Oh yeah, did you make it to New York?"

"Yeah, I just walked into my apartment. I'm about to get a shower and get dressed to go to this stupid, fucking charity event." I can hear the disdain in his voice.

I laugh. "That's not a nice way to talk about charity."

I hear his heavy breath blow across the phone. "I'd much rather be there with you. Hmmmm ..."

"What?" I can't hold back my grin. I don't know why, but that sounded like a very dirty hmmmm.

"That cheerleading uniform ..."

"Mmm-hmm."

"I want you to bring it over the next time you stay."

I laugh. "What?"

I can imagine him nodding his head vigorously. "Yeah, well ... Not so much the shorts that go under the skirt. But the skirt, for sure. The top too, although I'll probably rip that off."

I giggle. "You can't rip my top. It will take all season to get a new one made."

"Fine. Just the skirt, no panties, no top."

I roll my eyes. "Just a bra?"

"No, nothing up top. You can do a topless cheer for me."

I imagine it, and my blood warms.

"Damnit," he breathes out.

"What's wrong?"

"You and your topless cheer got me all excited."

I laugh. "You mean, your topless cheer? You're the one that brought it up."

"So, you're blaming this on me?"

"Absolutely. It's all on you."

"Well, maybe you can help me out then." I hear him lower his zipper.

"I sure will … As soon as you get back home."

He scoffs. "Seriously?"

I grin. "Yep."

He takes a deep breath. "How about a picture?"

"A picture?" I question.

"Yeah, something I can look at while I take care of this problem."

I laugh harder. "After all the dirty positions you've had me in, I think you have more than enough to work with."

I can hear his smile. "Yeah, you're probably right. I should go, get this shower, and get my night started."

"When are you coming back?"

"Tomorrow. You think you can wait that long?"

"I don't know …" I tease. "You make me wait much longer, and I'll be the one with the problem."

He moans. "What I wouldn't give to see that."

I grin. "We both know you'd just get jealous."

He laughs. "You're probably right. I'll talk to you later, gorgeous."

"Bye." I hang up the phone as a smile pulls at my lips. My heart is happy and racing.

Things are still new with Theo and I, but we have a connection that neither of us can deny. It's what pulled us together that first night. It's what made staying away from one another nearly impossible. And now that we've both given up on that whole *staying away from one another* thing, it's no longer just something invisible between us. Now, it's palpable. It's a part of me, just like my arm or leg. It's inside of me, somewhere between my heart and stomach, but it's felt in both places. It's deep, not easily forgotten about. It isn't like a liver or a kidney—something you don't even realize you have. It's like your heart, which you can feel beating. It's like your lungs, which you can feel taking in much-needed oxygen.

Whatever this is, it has control over every aspect of my body. When we see one another, it's what makes my heart race. It makes me feel breathless. It causes the goosebumps to prickle my skin, and it makes the butterflies in my stomach come alive. It's what causes that tingling sensation when he touches me. And it's what causes that explosion in my body when he pushes into me.

Just thinking of him has my blood boiling and my skin overheating. It's almost like I'm addicted to him now. He's the most dangerous drug for me—one that was created with my genetic makeup in mind. We were just together earlier in the day, yet I'm already missing the way those blue eyes watch me, the way his jaw tightens and his Adam's apple bobs. I miss his warm breath on my skin and the way shivers quake through my body when he kisses that one spot on my neck. I miss feeling his hands on me, his mouth. I miss the way my heart races when we're together, and I miss the way he makes me feel drunk without even needing a drink.

A sigh slips past my lips as I push myself up. I tell myself that he'll be home tomorrow, and there will be no separating us. Until then, I have more than enough to keep me busy. The first thing I need to do is get up and find myself some dinner because my stomach is starting to growl. So, I make my way toward the kitchen, and I make myself a grilled chicken breast that I season and slice up to top a salad with. I eat on the couch while watching TV, and then I do a little reading. When ten o'clock rolls around, I finally call it a night and head to bed.

I toss and turn for at least an hour before I give up and grab my phone from the dock on my bedside table. My fingers seem to have a mind of their own because the next thing I know, I'm on Theo's social media page, flipping through his pictures once again. Seeing him makes my heart race. I love his thick, dark hair and the way it feels when I run my fingers through it. He's friends with my dad, so of course, the two of us can't be friends. I'm thankful that his page is public, though. I love his wide smile in the photos he uses, how tan his skin looks to his bright, white teeth. I love the pictures when I can see his hands because I know all the talented things those hands can do.

I scroll through every picture, but I want so much more. I know what I really want is him here with me, but tonight … I'll have to settle with the pictures I find. And since I've combed through social media, I decide to switch to my internet app and look up his name. In the blink of an eye, I pull up thousands of pictures and articles about him. My heart flutters with excitement. I find articles from The New York Times, online magazines, and business websites. I click on one after the next, reading everything I can get my hands on. In doing so, I learn so much about him that I haven't had time to learn in person yet. Things such as his birthday, where he was born, and where he went to school.

After reading a few of the articles, I switch to the image section, and the first picture catches my attention. I'm not surprised to see how good-looking he is in the picture. I'm not surprised to see him climbing out of a limo or the fact that he's on the red carpet in an expensive-looking suit. I'm not even surprised to see the beautiful blonde woman on his arm. What surprises me is the date on the picture. It's today's date.

There has to be some mistake, right? I mean, Theo and I agreed that we wouldn't see other people. This picture was probably just posted today, but I'm sure it was taken months ago, probably before he ever moved here and met me.

I fall into a rabbit hole that leads me on a wild goose chase. I take the tips I get from the picture, and I follow them to the photographer's website. I don't find much there, but I do find another picture of the blonde woman, and it gives her name. Then I'm able to look her up. What I find only makes me feel more nervous because she isn't just some beautiful woman off the street. She's basically royalty.

She's the daughter of some wealthy architect who's responsible for building many of New York's skyscrapers. Of course, she's had her fair share of modeling and acting credits. She's well known in the charity world too, as it looks like she uses her fame for a good cause, starting charities and scholarships. She's famous, rich, and gorgeous. After doing my homework on her, I find that while she looks young—maybe only a few years older than me—she's actually Theo's age. In the picture of the two of them, it looks like they've just climbed out of that limo together. They're looking at one another with sparkling eyes and wide smiles. Her mouth is even slightly open, like he said something funny that made her laugh. I hate the way he's looking at her, as it reminds me of the way he looks at me. My heart drops to my stomach that is suddenly tied into knots.

It takes me another thirty minutes or so to figure out what charity event the two attended tonight, and once I have that, I type that information into YouTube, where I actually find a paparazzi video of the two arriving at tonight's event. I click play on the video, and my heart pounds.

It's dark, and I can hear the faint background noise of the city. There's a large group of people behind the red velvet ropes, all of them watching the limos that are pulling up to the carpet. Limo after limo pulls up, and the perfect couples step out. The men are dressed in all black. The women are wearing beautiful formal dresses. They're dripping in gold and diamonds, and all of them have flawless hair and makeup. If I didn't know any better, I'd think this was a movie premiere—only I don't know the people who are climbing out of these limos. They're famous and rich, clearly, but they're famous in their own little community of the business world—the rich world that I'm not involved in.

Finally, I see Theo step out of a limo. He offers a woman his hand, and he helps her out. This beautiful, angel-like woman steps out of the limo and stands at his side. They both glance toward the crowd, and then he looks back at her. He says something I can't hear, and she laughs. This is the moment that picture is capturing. They look this way and that, getting picture after picture, and finally, he holds out his elbow. She wraps her hand around it, and he leads her away. The video goes on to show other couples, but I swipe it away.

I put my phone away and roll over, wanting to force myself to sleep, but sleep doesn't come. What does come are all my insecurities. I think about how beautiful that woman is, and I think of how he looked at her. I think of how she's much more fitting for him than I am. I mean, she's rich and famous. She's his own age. They are both involved in the same charities. What do Theo and I have in common?

Not only do they look great together, but they're also a much better fit than he and I will ever be. He isn't her professor. He isn't friends with her father—that I know of. He doesn't have to hide being with her, and that makes things much easier. How long is he going to want to go out of his way to be with me? Eventually, he's going to get tired of hiding. He's going to get bored, never being able to leave the house like in a normal relationship. He tried telling me. He tried warning me, but I refused to listen. Now, it's abundantly clear.

He and I … it can't work.

The whole world is against us.

And in the end, I'm going to be the one getting hurt, while he's the one moving on to the next beautiful woman who's throwing herself at him, just like I've been doing.

THEO

"So, tell me all about this woman you're being so secretive about," Zoe says as she sits across the table from me at the charity event we're attending.

I chuckle, bringing my drink to my lips and taking a sip. "Who says there's a woman?"

She rolls her blue eyes as she offers up a tight smirk. "You act like we haven't known one another since birth, Theo. All I have to do is look in your eyes and see that there's a woman."

I scoff as I sit back in my chair.

She leans forward. "You're not typically a happy person. That's not a bad thing. Some people are naturally positive. Some are naturally negative. And then, some people like you, you're neutral. You wake up in this neutral headspace all day, and you act accordingly. If you have a good morning, you'll look more pleasant. If you have a bad morning, you usually look downright pissed off. But this ..." she motions toward me with her index finger. "This is neither. This is a look of genuine happiness, and I know you well enough to know that means you've met someone in Chicago. So, tell me about her."

I laugh and shake my head, taking a sip of my whiskey. I lean forward. "Alright, but you have to keep your mouth shut because if this gets out, it will be one hell of a mess."

She nods. "You know I'd never breathe a word of anything we talk about."

I wet my lips, and my heart begins to race. She's right. Kaylee is making me unbelievably happy, and I've been dying to talk to someone about it. "The first weekend I was in Chicago, I went out to a club. I needed out of the house, and I wanted to grab a drink. I hoped to meet someone to keep me company for the night."

She nods me on.

"Well, I met someone." I take a deep breath, remembering the way she made me feel the moment our eyes met for the first time. "I was up in VIP. She was on the floor below, but there's a balcony that overlooks the lower level. I was leaning against the ledge, sipping my drink, and watching everyone dance. My eyes met hers, and I felt every hair stand on end. Every muscle in my body flexed, and my blood started to boil. The two of us watched one another for some time before I finally went down to introduce myself. And we hit it off. We had a couple of drinks, flirted, talked, danced. And then we kissed, and it felt like I got struck by lightning. I took her back to my place and ... Well, let's just say it's a night I'll never forget."

She smiles. "That's awesome, Theo. It's about time you finally met someone you can see yourself with for longer than a weekend." She laughs.

I nod. "Right. I was excited too. The only problem was that she was gone before I woke up."

She gasps, and her brows lift.

"I was trying to figure out a way to find out who she was, how I could reach her. All I had was her first name. I didn't know her last name, didn't have her number. Then, I go to the university for my first day of work."

She gasps, putting it together. "No," she breathes out, wide-eyed.

I nod. "Yep, you guessed it. I walked into class, and there she is, sitting right in front of me, just as surprised as I was."

She shakes her head and massages her brows.

"To top it all off, she's the daughter of the friend who invited me to the university in the first place."

Her mouth drops open. "This girl, she has to be what … at least twenty years younger than you?"

"Eighteen," I correct. "Asher got his high school girlfriend pregnant their senior year."

"So … what? How?"

I take another drink of my whiskey. "I avoided her on campus. I refused to look at her. Wouldn't talk to her if it could be avoided. I was determined to put that night behind me and forget it happened. It was the only right thing to do, right?"

She doesn't agree or disagree. She just sits, watching and listening to my story.

"The thing is, though ..." I chuckle. "There's something about her that I can't resist. No matter what I did, I couldn't stop myself from thinking about her. I could ignore her on campus, but then I'd go home and dream of her. Every day I resisted the pull she had on me, it only got stronger. Then, we had it out in class one day. I told her it wasn't going to happen again, that she needed to move on and forget it. She showed up at my apartment that night. One thing led to another, and ..." I hold my hand in the air and let it fall back to the table.

I finish off my drink and push the glass away. "The thing is, neither of us want to stop. So the only option we have is to hide our relationship for the next year. She's graduating, and I'll be moving back here. She doesn't seem to be bothered by the fact that this is something her father probably won't approve of, but ..." I shrug.

"And what about you?"

"What about me?"

"I mean, are you worried about what her father will think? You said you two have been friends for many years now. If he doesn't approve, you'll be losing a friend."

I nod. "Honestly, I haven't thought much about it yet. This is all still new. Asher and I, we haven't really been close for many years now. Honestly, if he no longer wanted to be friends, I don't think my life would change much."

She flags down the waiter, and he brings us both over a fresh drink. "Well, this girl must be really special if you're going through all the trouble to keep it quiet." She sips her wine. "Have you two talked about the future?"

I sip my drink. "Not much, but I know she's looking for a career in writing. So, I'm thinking at the end of the school year, the two of us will move back here together. She can stay with me. I can even find her a job on one of the magazines. Of course, I'd understand if she wants to pave her own way in the industry as well."

"And you think this can work with the two of you? I mean, with so many years between you …"

I nod as I turn my eyes down to my drink. "She's different. I don't know how or why. But I know I've never felt like this with anyone else. That has to mean something, right?"

She offers a smile and nods. "Yeah, I guess it does." Then she shrugs both shoulders, and her grin spreads. "When do I get to meet her?"

I laugh. "Don't hold your breath."

* * *

The charity event goes by smoothly for the most part. We all donate money, pose for pictures, and drink more than we should. When the night ends, the limo drops Zoe off first, and then I'm taken home. I make my way up to my penthouse apartment, and I strip out of my stuffy suit. I have a good buzz going, so I climb straight into bed, hoping to get some rest. I turn off the lights and close my eyes. The first person I see behind my lids is her. I remember watching her sleep in my arms. I remember the way her dark hair was splayed across my white pillows. I studied her face, wanting to burn every aspect into my memory. Things such as the way her long, black lashes were fanned across her cheeks. How relaxed her facial muscles were. The curvature of her lips; the top lip arches high with sharp points, while her bottom lip is curvy and thicker. I remember how sweet they taste. How soft they are when I feel them against mine or wrapped around my dick.

I groan when I feel my cock start to come alive. I don't know what it is about this woman, but I can't get enough. It only makes me want to get up right now and climb on the redeye so I can get back to her that much faster. The only problem is that I don't know where she lives, so I wouldn't be able to go to her. She also has a roommate, so I couldn't go to her, even if I did know where she lives. I hate hiding, and I hate sneaking around. I hate that nobody knows that she belongs to me. But it's what I'll do if it means keeping her.

I open my eyes, seeing nothing but a bright blue sky above, white puffy clouds, and the blinding sun. I smell the salt in the air, and I hear the way the ocean is lapping at the sides of the yacht. I'm warm, as I'm lying in the sun. I'm happy, my heart never feeling as full. My life is perfect. Finally, I'm getting everything I've ever wanted.

Kay's smiling face comes into view. She climbs onto my deckchair, straddling me. My hands move to her thighs as my eyes take her in. She's only wearing her white string bikini. Her skin is sun-kissed and golden, and her dark hair is full of waves, falling around her gorgeous face naturally.

"It's about time you woke up. Are you ready to get this show on the road?"

I sit up, capturing her lips with mine. They're soft, sweet, making me yearn for so much more. "I've been ready," I whisper against them.

She pulls back with a smile. "Good. Let's get on with it. Then we can start to focus on the next section of this little vacation." She climbs off of me, but she takes my hand, pulling me to my feet. Then she leads me to the bow of the yacht, where our minister is already waiting. Today, I make her mine. Today, she takes my last name. And after today, there's nothing he can do to take her away from me. I may have stolen her from him, but this process is going to legally make her mine, and once she's mine, I'll never let her go.

The ceremony is only for us. It is a moment we refuse to share with anyone else. The whole thing only takes fifteen minutes, and the moment I'm told I can kiss my bride, I pull her against me, our mouths welding together. Picking her up, I waste no time in taking her down to the lower levels, to the bedroom we've been using.

I untie her top, and it falls between us. I kick the door shut as my hands tug at the strings on her hips. When her bottoms fall away, I lay her down on the bed before me. My eyes start on hers, and they fall down her body, nice and slow. Her breathing is already labored, and I haven't even touched her yet. It's causing her chest to rise and fall quickly. I watch the way her dusty-pink nipples harden, and I lick my lips, ready to eat her up.

"What are you waiting for?" She grins.

I push my swim shorts down my hips, and I crawl onto the bed. She wraps her arms around my neck, and her knees lift into the air so my hips settle between them, right where I belong.

"How in the hell did I get so lucky?" I ask her, cupping her jaw while looking into her eyes.

She smiles and shrugs. "Maybe I'm the one who got lucky." She pulls me down for a kiss, and the moment our lips touch ...

My alarm goes off, pulling me from my dreams. I groan and turn off the alarm, instantly pissed that I've been pulled away from her once again—real or not. I want her all to myself. I want to be able to look at her for as long as I want. I want to be able to reach out and touch her, kiss her without it causing alarm. I want to spend the rest of my life with her, and I don't want anyone to ever come between us. I'm more than ready to live for her. I wonder if she wants to live for me?

I shake the thoughts from my head. I'm not sure when I'll be able to have her all to myself, but I know that right now, I need to get up so I can make my way back to her. Seeing her and not being able to touch her is better than only having her in a dream. A sigh slips from my lips as I throw back the blanket.

I shower, dress, and head out. Since I cleaned out the food before moving to Chicago, I have no choice but to go out for breakfast and coffee, but that's okay because I have plenty of time to kill before my flight anyway. I go to my favorite restaurant, and I order myself an omelet and some coffee. While I wait, I pull out my phone and give her a call, wanting to hear her voice before getting on that plane. Her phone rings and rings before getting picked up by voicemail. I don't leave a message just because I don't want it to end up in the wrong hands. Feeling bummed, I hang up the phone.

I try calling again when I land that afternoon, but there's still no answer. I try not to let it bother me as I go about with my day. When she still doesn't answer that evening, I start to worry. Is she okay? Is she hurt? Did something happen? Is she avoiding me? Did I do something to make her avoid me? The last I knew, everything was great, and she was wishing I was home. How can one go from wanting someone around to not wanting to talk to them at all?

Sunday passes slowly. So fucking slowly, but there's nothing I can do other than wait for her to call me back or to answer her phone when I call. I have no idea how else to get ahold of her. Worse comes to worse, I'll see her on campus on Monday. I just have to make it that long.

By the time Monday rolls around, I'm like a junkie who hasn't had a hit. I'm nervous and anxious. I leave early, knowing damn well I won't have anything to do on campus, but I have to see her. I have to see if she's okay.

KAYLEE

I've ignored him all weekend. In fact, I haven't even left my apartment all weekend in fear of running into him somewhere. I know he's looking for an explanation, but I just need time to think. On one hand, the picture I saw could be completely innocent. I mean, it's not like they were touching, or kissing, or anything. On the other hand, why didn't he tell me about her? If it were nothing, he would have no reason to try and hide it. And then again, what in the hell does he want with me when he can have a woman like that? It only reminds me that the two of us have very little in common. I'm just a college student. I haven't even finished my education. I'm not flourishing in my career. I don't have my own place, and I'm not rich or famous. What does he even see in me?

Eventually, Monday rolls around, and I know I'm finally going to have to see him. The only thing is, I still haven't figured out what I should say, if I should say anything at all. I don't want to be the kind of girl who freaks out when he's away and then forgets it all the moment he's back. I need answers, but this is still so new that I'm not sure he even owes me anything. Do I have a right to ask who the woman was, and why he didn't warn me about her ahead of time? It's not like he's been checking in to make sure I'm not with Xander. He's sure of himself. I... am not.

I see him a few times throughout the day on campus. Every time, I refuse to look his way. Instead, I watch him from the corner of my eye, and I can see him willing me to look at him. His eyes are drilling into my skull, pleading with me to look at him. I hold strong, and I never do. I consider skipping my afternoon at the paper just to avoid seeing him, but it's Monday, so new assignments are going out. If I miss today, I won't have an assignment for the week, and I can't go all week without something to do.

I walk into the newsroom, and I see his brows lift the second I walk into the room. I take my seat, and he leans forward at his desk, almost like he's getting as close to me as he can. I feel his eyes boring into my head, and my blood warms with his attention on me. I keep my eyes trained on my desk until I get my next assignment, and instead of hanging out and getting to work on it, I hightail it out of class, planning on working on it at home, where he will be unable to look at me. I practically sprint through the hallways, and I'm nearly breathless by the time I push my way out the door. Outside, I suck in a deep breath, hearing nothing but the sound of my heart beating. My stomach tightens as I walk down the sidewalk. I feel every hair stand on end, and I know he's followed me out. A quick glance over my shoulder is proof enough. He's matching me step for step, always keeping the same amount of space between us. His hands are clenched into fists at his sides.

I pray that he stops at the coffee cart as I pass it. A few steps later, I glance back, finding him still behind me. The problem is that there's no place we can talk without being seen by someone. Not knowing what else to do, I continue on my way to the parking lot. The closer I get to my car at the back of the lot, the faster my legs move. I'm reaching for the door handles when he grabs my wrist and spins me around.

I gasp as he pushes my back against the side of my car. His hand tangles into my hair, cupping the back of my head as his mouth crashes into mine. The butterflies start to flutter their wings, flying around my body, and my muscles tighten in response to his forcefulness, which I love. If he never breaks this kiss, I could be happy here forever. I could forget about last weekend, and nothing would ever change between us. But the kiss has to end eventually.

He slows the kiss, and he nips my lower lip before pulling back. My eyes open and lock on his. "Fuck, I've missed you," he breathes out, his hands moving up to cup my face as he starts to move back in.

For a split second, I almost allow it, but then I feel that knife in my chest like it's been twisted, and I pull back while pushing him away.

His face contorts into confusion and then pain. "What's going on, Kaylee?"

I shake my head, not wanting to think the words, let alone say them.

His hand cups my jaw, his thumb gently sweeping back and forth across my lower lip. "What happened, beautiful?" He leans in, kissing my lips softly. "Last we talked, you couldn't wait for me to get back. Now you're avoiding me and refusing to even look at me. What happened, Kaylee?" His blue eyes are pleading with me to explain.

I pull my phone out of my back pocket, and I swipe the lock screen away. Then I open my web browser—the picture is still on the screen. Pain slices through my chest just from looking at it again, but I turn the phone around so he can see the picture.

He falls back a step as confusion pinches his face. His eyes move from mine down to the phone in my hand. He sees what I've been staring at all weekend, and then acknowledgment washes over him. He's no longer confused. He no longer looks upset. Now, he looks guilty.

"I can explain," he starts, but I shake my head as I open my car door.

"Save it for the next naive girl that falls for your shit." I slide into the driver's seat, and I close the door. As quickly as I can, I toss my things into the passenger seat, and I push the button on the dash to start the engine. I pull on my seatbelt while trying to ignore the way he's knocking on my window and begging me to stop. Shifting into drive, I pull away as quickly as I can.

My eyes fill with tears as I drive away, but I'm proud of myself. I held my ground and stood up for myself, even when I could have melted into him and that kiss. I don't want things to end like this, but he's not the guy I thought he was.

Turns out, he's just another player, looking to sleep with as many women as he can. That kind of ruins my hopes and dreams for the future. I've always been told that girls mature faster than boys, so I hoped a man of his age would be more mature than the guy who sits next to me in class. I guess that isn't the case. Maybe sleeping around isn't something a man can outgrow. Maybe it's just in their blood, in their DNA to spread their seed as much as humanly possible.

I make it home, and I waste no time going inside. I ride the elevator up, and then I rush down the hall and let myself into the apartment. I'm glad that Margo isn't home. I don't want a million questions right now. I can't explain this anyway. Dropping my bag onto the kitchen table, I open the fridge to get a soda. That's when the knock on the door gets my attention. I don't know why, but my stomach fills with tingles.

Closing the fridge, I slowly move to the door. I wrap my hand around the knob, and I pull it open, finding Theo on the other side.

"Please, let me explain."

"Did you follow me here?"

"I had no choice. You won't answer your phone, and you refuse to even look at me on campus. Just let me in. Let me explain. If by the end you still hate me, I'll leave, and you won't even have to ask me to."

I guess it's the least I can do: let him explain. All I want to do is make him feel as bad as I did when I saw that picture. I'm sure I can do just that by shutting the door in his face and refusing to talk to him. But if that's what I really want to do, why do I find myself opening the door wider for him?

He steps into the kitchen and walks straight through to the living room, where his pacing begins. I step into the living room, and I lean my shoulder against the wall as I cross my arms over my chest.

He turns to face me. "I had that charity event planned for months, Kaylee. I was just an escort to a very old friend of mine. She and I, we've never been anything more than friends."

I roll my eyes. "You really expect me to believe that?"

"You have no reason to believe I'm lying." He points at his chest. "Have you ever caught me in a lie?"

He knows I haven't, so I turn my head away from him.

"I was invited to this event." He steps toward me. "I used to attend a lot of these things when I was living in New York. It's good exposure for my company. I go, the cause gets people's attention, and then someone writes about it, in turn giving my company attention. Then I make a big donation, and it's a tax write-off. It's a stupid, boring process, and I fucking hate it, but it's good for business."

"Why did you have to take her? And why didn't you tell me? Warn me?"

"You're given so many seats, and you're expected to fill them. I couldn't go alone, even if I wanted to. And I didn't tell you because … Well, honestly, I didn't even think about it. It never crossed my mind. I knew there wasn't anything going on, so to me, it was completely innocent. Now, looking back, I can see my mistake."

My eyes move back to his. "How would you like it if you left for a weekend and came back to see a picture of Xander and me together that the paper is printing? How would you like that?"

His jaw flexes. "I wouldn't like it at all."

A long breath leaves me. "You could've taken me to this event if you just needed to fill a chair."

He steps toward me. "I would have loved to, but this was a very public event, and we can't be seen together." His hands move to my arms. They slide down, holding my hands in his.

I bite my lower lip, knowing he has a point. "So, this woman …"

"Is just a friend. Her name is Zoe. Our fathers were friends, so we were together a lot growing up. We've never dated. We've never slept together. We've never even kissed. We're just friends. In fact, I spent the whole night talking about you."

I look into his eyes. "You did?"

He nods. "I did."

My anger is melting away. I don't know if I should believe him, but I want to. I shake my head and laugh. "How can you want me after being around a gorgeous woman like that? All the models you've dated. The actresses. I'm just a normal girl."

His hand cups my jaw. "There's nothing normal about you, beautiful." He leans in, his mouth pressing against mine. He kisses me softly and slowly, and I don't hold back this time.

He's right. I don't have a reason to assume he's lying. I can't do anything but believe him. For the first time since he left, I know without a shadow of a doubt that we were made to be together. I know because I can feel it.

Our kiss grows in speed and intensity, and the next thing I know, he's picking me up against him. I wrap my arms and legs around him, letting him carry me through the living room and into the hallway.

"Where's your room, gorgeous?" he asks against my lips.

"To your right," I respond, refusing to stop kissing him.

He turns to his right, and he carries me through my bedroom door. Spinning around, he is pressing my back against the door, effectively shutting it. Keeping me pinned between him and the door frees up his hands. I hear him twist the lock, and then his hands are back on me. Our kiss gets harder, faster. His hands are teasing, touring, massaging, kneading, and pulling away clothes.

It doesn't take long before we're both completely naked. Holding me against him, he moves us over to the bed. I'm not sure how he manages it—I must've blacked out. The next thing I know, I'm on my knees while my hands grip the headboard in front of me. My legs are spread while he lays on his back, his head between my thighs. His hands are holding and squeezing my ass, rocking my hips back and forth against his face, while his mouth works me closer and closer to the edge.

I'm so close to shattering that I can't even panic about the position I'm in right now. While I've enjoyed oral sex on several occasions, I've never been seated on someone's face before. Before, I worried that the guy would suffocate, that the position would make me feel exposed and nervous. Now, I can't do anything but rock my hips faster and faster.

My orgasm builds and builds inside my body. I hold it back as long as I can, knowing the longer I hold out, the higher I'll go. I no longer have an option when he slides two fingers into me. My orgasm goes ripping through my body, and I scream, cry, and beg for so much more. He doesn't relent until he's pushed me over every single wave of my release.

He slides out from under me, and I'm so weak, I'm afraid to move. I'm holding onto the headboard for dear life, breathing hard, and trying to recover from my near out-of-body experience. I feel him between my thighs, and then he's shoving into me, his chest against my back. My head falls back against his shoulder, and his hand moves to my chin, turning my head so his mouth can meet mine. I can taste myself on his lips, on his tongue, and I love that he's claimed by me. I love that he's willing to claim me, to completely fucking own me. And I'm glad that he's willing to prove himself to me in whatever way it takes. I don't know if we'll last forever, but I know now that we're both willing to try, and that means more than anything ever has.

THEO

My hands tighten on her hips. I thrust up as I pull her in place. I rock her against me, and she lets out a moan as her head falls back. I lean in, catching her nipple in my mouth. My tongue runs circles around it, flicks against it while my mouth sucks. Her hands are on the headboard, holding her upper body off of me. It lets her tits bounce before my eyes, and it leaves them exposed to my mouth. There's no part of her I leave untouched. My dark angel has me under her spell completely now, and there's no other way I'd have it.

My left hand moves between us, and I start to rub against her clit as I thrust up into her. Her breathing gets harder, and her moans get louder. I feel her walls starting to tighten around me, and I know she's close to coming undone. I know when she shatters, she'll pull me over the edge with her—I'm ready to explode already.

I thrust harder, and my hand moves faster. The closer we get to our release, the faster I move. She shatters on top of me, and she comes so fucking hard that she leaves a mess all over me and the bed. It's the sexiest fucking thing I've ever seen, and as I predicted, I go diving over that edge along with her. My hips take on a life of their own, going at the pace I need to ride out every wave of my release. I spill myself into her until I have nothing left. My hips slow to a stop, and she collapses against me. I wrap my arms around her, holding her tight as we both work to regain control over our bodies.

After several minutes of us recovering, she slides off of me and to my side, but I keep my arm around her, holding her to my side.

"We still have some things to figure out, you know?"

I roll to my side so I can face her. "Let's do it."

Her brows lift. "Like, right now?"

I nod.

"Okay …" Her eyes fill with nervousness.

"We both know that we have to keep this secret until the end of the school year. As much as I hate it, that much hasn't changed."

She nods.

"But when the school year does come to an end, I won't be staying here for another year. I plan on going back to New York, and I want you to go with me."

She smiles. "You do?"

"You can stay with me. I'll give you a job at the magazine if you want. I mean, I understand you wanting to pave your own way, but at least if I offered you a job, you'd have an excuse to give your dad as to why you're moving to New York to begin with. There, we won't have to hide. You'll be all mine." I lean in, peppering her jaw and neck with kisses.

She laughs and wiggles against me until I pull back. She settles and moves her eyes back to mine. "This is still so new. Do you think it's okay that we make these plans now? I mean, aren't you worried that it's too soon?"

"I've never been sure of anything in my life. Until I met you. I can't imagine ever letting you walk away from me, Kay. I need to know that you'll be here, by my side, for the rest of my life. I want to know that I'll have you in my bed every single night. I need to know that I'll get to wake up to your beautiful face every single morning. I'm a greedy man, Kay. I don't like to share. And I don't want to share you with the world. I want you to be all mine for the rest of our lives." I lean in, pressing my mouth to hers.

Her fingers lace into my hair, and she pulls me closer as she deepens the kiss. I hate that she was filled with doubt before. If I could go back and do things differently, I would go back and tell her about Zoe. Hell, I'd even take her to New York with me so the two could have met. There's never going to be another woman in my life. Kay is the most important person in the world to me, and it kills me that I almost lost her over a misunderstanding like this. Just thinking of having to let her go causes a sharp pain to slice through my chest.

She pulls me on top of her, and my hips slide between her thighs. I can feel the junction between her legs, still swollen and slick from our lovemaking.

"Theo," she breathes out.

"What is it, Kay?" I pull back so I can look into her eyes.

Her hooded green eyes open and lock on mine. "I know this is crazy, but I ..." She bites her lower lip.

I cup her jaw. "What is it, gorgeous?"

Her green eyes blazer hotter. "I love you. I know it's early. I know it's fast and insane. But I love you."

My heart starts to pound in my chest, and it feels like the air has been sucked from my lungs. "I love you too, angel." My mouth crashes against hers, and her hold on me only tightens. She wiggles her hips and grinds against me until I'm hard for her all over again. I slide into her body with ease, as she's still slick and coated in my earlier release. I swear, if we could stay like this for the rest of our lives, we would. In her arms, lost in her eyes, buried in her body, this is heaven to me, and I've never seen anything that was more beautiful.

Someone pats me on the shoulder.

I turn to see Asher come to a stop at my side. "I bet you're one happy father today, aren't you?"

He looks at his daughter, who's dressed in her cap and gown. His eyes get a little misty. "I've never been more proud of her."

I turn back to the graduating class and smile, keeping my eyes on her. Somehow, the two of us managed to keep this relationship of ours a secret for all these months. Now that things are coming to an end, it's almost time for the next step in our plan, and neither of us can wait to finally be out in the world where we no longer have to hide.

"Thank you for giving her that job, by the way. I know it means a lot to her, and it eases my mind knowing that she'll be able to take care of herself."

"You don't have to thank me, Ash. She did all the work herself. She's a good writer, and I'm happy to have her join the team."

He smiles, nods, and pats my shoulder. "Anything I can do to talk you into another year here?"

I laugh and shake my head. "No, I don't think so. The paper is doing well, and it's time I get back to my real life in the city. Plus, I have a few new employees that I need to make sure are being trained right."

He smiles and nods. "Well, anytime you change your mind, I'm just a call away. This job will be yours at the drop of a hat." He offers his hand to shake.

"Thank you." I shake his hand, and then I watch him go walking toward his daughter with his arms extended. They hug, and she smiles at me from over his shoulder. I'm happy that she's enjoying her big day, but I can't wait to get her in New York, where I'll no longer have to share her.

Her father, stepmother, and her mother all take her out for a big family dinner to celebrate her graduation. As much as I wish I could be a part of it, I stay home, making sure I get everything packed up for the move. Luckily, I don't have to worry about the furniture, as the place came furnished. I still have a lot to pack when it comes to my office and bedroom, though.

I'm in the bedroom when I hear the front door shut.

"Theo?" she calls out.

"In the bedroom," I reply, closing a box and pushing it aside.

She walks into the room, and she tosses her cap and gown to the side. "Wow, you've gotten a lot done." She glances around the room.

"How was dinner?"

She kicks off her shoes and starts unbuttoning the front of her dress. "Fine, I guess. There was no fighting or bickering, even with the three of them together, so that was good. The whole time, I just watched the clock so I could come back here. I wanted to help you pack." Her dress falls from her arms, leaving her in nothing but a black bra and matching panties. "But it looks like you have everything covered. You going to be ready to catch our flight tomorrow?"

"Everything is packed, but the last few things we'll toss into our bags in the morning." I grab her hip and pull her chest to mine. "Looks like we have the whole night to ourselves. How do you want to spend it?"

She wraps her arms around my shoulders. "Hmmmm ... First, a long, hot shower, where you wash my hair and body."

I grin, walking her backward toward the open bathroom door.

"Then, of course, we can end the shower with one of those earth-shattering orgasms you always give me."

My grin turns to a smile as we step into the bathroom.

"Then I'm thinking ice cream on the couch while we relax and watch a little TV. Of course, you're more than welcome to massage my feet that are sore from being crammed into those heels all day long."

"Oh, I'm more than welcome to?" I challenge, unhooking her bra.

She grins and nods. "Mmm-hmm." She pulls her arms from the straps. "And then, if you're lucky, I'll let you fuck me into exhaustion before drifting off to sleep."

"You drive a hard bargain," I tease, pulling her mouth to mine.

I pick her up and carry her to the shower. Stepping in, she tips her head back so I can wet her hair. I work some shampoo into her locks, and then I rinse before rubbing every inch of her down with some of my favorite body wash. Once she's good and clean and more than primed up from our teasing shower, I position her foot on the built-in bench, exposing her center.

Her eyes open, a fire burning in them, as she wonders what I'm going to do.

I smirk as my hand moves between her legs. My fingers rub against her clit until she's wet enough that they can slide inside. Her head falls back against the shower wall, and her breathing gets harder as her hands tighten on my shoulders.

"I don't think I'm going to come like this, Theo. Even though it feels good, I need more."

"What are you saying?" My hand moves faster, my fingers thrusting into her while my palm grinds against her clit.

A whimper falls from her lips. "I want you inside of me."

"I am inside of you."

She shakes her head. "No. I want this." She wraps her hand around my dick. When my Adam's apple bobs from her touch, she starts working me from base to tip.

"You want that?" My eyes glance down. "You're going to have to work for it." A grin tugs at my lips.

Her brow arches. "And how am I supposed to do that?"

"You're not getting my dick, Kay. Not until you come on my fingers."

She bites her lower lip. "I don't know if I can. You have me too spoiled for that." She offers a sexy grin.

"You can and you will." I thrust my fingers into her faster, harder—my palm grinding against her clit. "I know this greedy little pussy better than you do, Kay. I know any attention from me will have you riding anything you can for relief. Right now, I want you riding my fingers, and I want you to come. I want you to make a fucking mess, gorgeous." Her eyes are already rolling back, and her chest is rising and falling faster. "Can you do that for me, baby? Can you come on my fingers to get my dick in that greedy pussy of yours?"

Her eyes are shut, lips parted with her heavy breathing, but she nods as I feel her body tightening against mine.

My hand keeps going. "I know you're getting close, Kay. I know you want to come right now, so you can have me inside you, but you have to hold it back." I bite her neck and then her ear. "Hold it back and let it grow bigger and bigger. It's the only way you'll make a mess for me."

Her moans get louder, echoing off the tile walls of the bathroom.

"Not yet, Kay. Hold it back."

She digs her nails into my shoulders, and I take a hissing breath.

"Not yet."

Her legs are growing weak. and they're starting to shake.

"Now, angel. Come on my fingers. Show me how badly you want me inside you."

She lets her orgasm go, and her moans and screams only get louder, echoing all around us as she does exactly what I tell her to. Her release comes squirting out of her body, and it makes me want her so fucking bad that my cock hurts. Withdrawing my hand from between her legs, I take hold of and position myself at her entrance. I thrust my hips upward and slide into her tight little body, which I know was made only for me. It only makes her release last that much longer, and she squirts her excitement all over me.

Her muscles are quivering around my cock in ways I didn't know they could move, and she's holding onto me for dear life while I thrust into her hard and fast like I'm pressed for time, like I'm chasing after the only orgasm I'll ever have. Normally, I'd be ashamed to admit how fast she can make me come, but this is only the pre-show, and we both know it. I dive over the edge of the cliff with her, filling her with my come and giving her everything I have until I'm too weak to move another muscle.

KAYLEE

"Sometimes, I still can't believe I'm here," I say into the phone as I look out at the beautiful New York skyline.

"I still can't believe you didn't tell me that you were banging it out with your professor," Margo teases, making me roll my eyes.

I laugh. "I told you. He wasn't exactly a professor. And I couldn't tell you. There was too much riding on it to risk it getting out. It's not that I didn't trust you, it's just that—"

"I know, I know. I'm just giving you shit." She laughs out loud. "But seriously … you bagged yourself one of the hottest, richest men in the state of New York. I feel like an *atta girl* is in order." I can hear her clapping and whistling.

I laugh.

"So, it's getting pretty close to five o'clock. What does this evening hold in store for you?"

I check the time on my watch. "Oh, not much. Theo and I are just planning on going out and grabbing some dinner. We almost never eat at home anymore. We spent a year hiding behind closed doors. Now that we don't have to hide anymore, we're out as much as we can be."

"Oh, fancy date night with the hottie? Ugh, I'm so jealous; it makes me sick."

"Margs … things will turn around for you."

"When?" she questions.

"Any day now," I promise.

Margo had big dreams of moving to New York with me. We saw ourselves living glamorous lives just like on *Sex in the City*. I found my prince charming, but Margo … She didn't get so lucky. As she was packing up her side of our apartment, she ended up getting a call that changed everything. Her father passed away, leaving her in charge of his estate. Instead of joining me in New York, she had to go back home to southern Illinois. To say she's struggling with handling it all is an understatement.

I can almost hear her rolling her eyes. "I'm holding you to that. If things don't turn around for me in a month, I'm coming to New York to kick your butt for breaking your promise."

I laugh. "Deal. And while you're here, we can catch up and have dinner too."

She sighs. "I miss you."

"I miss you too." I smile, even though she isn't here to see it.

"I should get back to work. Call me later."

"Bye." I hang up the phone and turn my attention back to the window, looking down at the busy street that never seems to slow down.

It's been three months since Theo and I officially moved to New York. I took my time getting settled into his apartment, and we had somewhat of a honeymoon phase as he made room for me and all my things. Then, he brought me into the office and introduced me as his girlfriend, who just moved to the city to work together.

I was prepared for jealous women to come at me, but to my surprise, everyone has been extremely welcoming. Theo also hired a couple of other students from the newspaper to join the magazine here in New York. Both of them, however, are working for the men's magazine while I'm working for the women's, so as far as I know, neither of them are aware that I ended up being involved with the man who was a part of our college staff—not that anything can be done about it now.

I turn away from the window and move back to my desk to gather my things. I shut down my computer for the night, and I log out of the phone system so all calls will go to voicemail. I turn off my desk lamp, and I'm standing when Theo walks into my office. He sees me, and his eyes light up as a smile tugs at his lips.

"Ready for me?"

I grin. "I'm always ready for you."

He shuts the door and steps toward me, his hand going to his belt. "You may want to rephrase that sentence because the way you said it has dirty thoughts running through my head."

I laugh, putting my hand on his chest. "I am ready to go home." I tilt my head back so I can look into those blazing blue eyes of his. "Better?"

"Yes and no," he says, his hand moving up to cup my jaw. He leans in, capturing my mouth with his. His lips are strong but soft as he kisses me. Even though we've been living together for three months now, even though we've been dating for over a year, I still get butterflies in my stomach when he touches me. All it takes is a look from him to have my blood boiling with need.

I lace my fingers into his hair, pulling him closer as I deepen our kiss. He allows it to go on for a moment, but he pulls back and gives me a warning look. "Don't tease me, angel. You know that door doesn't lock, and I'd hate for someone to walk in while I was fucking you over that desk." That fire erupts in his eyes.

"I guess we better get home then." I offer him a sexy grin.

He falls back a step, laughing while shaking his head. "You're going to kill me one of these days." He pulls my door open.

I laugh as I step out ahead of him, leading the way to the elevator.

Here in the city, there isn't really a need to drive if it can be avoided. The traffic is terrible, not to mention that parking costs are astronomical. Instead of driving ourselves, Theo pays for a car to take us to and from work every day. Any time we need to drive on nights or weekends, he drives us, or we just grab a taxi. By the time we're stepping out of the building, our car is already parked against the curb. Theo pulls open the door for me, and I slide in with him climbing in behind me.

The car drops us off outside of our building, and we climb out and make our way to the top floor. Theo unlocks the door for us, and he holds it open, allowing me to walk in ahead of him. "What sounds good tonight?"

I stop at the entryway table, putting down my purse as I turn to him. "I picked last night. It's your turn to pick."

He wraps his arms around my waist. "I don't care what I eat, as long as I have you sitting across from me."

I giggle. "That was so cheesy."

He shrugs. "It's true." He leans in for a quick kiss.

It doesn't take much for him to convince me to narrow down our options. "You want something fancy, or you want to put on some normal clothes and grab something greasy that we can eat in comfort?"

His brows pull together as he thinks it over. "When you put it like that, unhealthy and comfort win every time."

I giggle. "Pizza it is then." I kiss him once more. "Come on. Let's get out of these stuffy clothes." I release him and spin around to make my way to our bedroom.

He follows me through the apartment and into the bedroom, where we each go to our own walk-in closet. I kick off my shoes and put them back on the shelf, and then I work on removing my belt and putting it away. I unfasten my skirt and let it fall onto the floor. Finally, I pull off my button-up shirt, tossing both items into the laundry basket.

"I got a call from Asher today," Theo says from his closet. He still refuses to call him my father.

"Oh yeah? What did he want?" I pull open a drawer and pull out a pair of jeans.

He appears in the doorway of my closet, still wearing his dress pants, but his button-up shirt is gone. His pants are unbuttoned and unzipped, giving me one hell of a view. "He and Meredith are in the city, taking a little trip before school starts up next week. He wanted to know if I wanted to meet up with them."

I toss my jeans to the bench in the center of the room as I dig for a shirt. "And what did you tell him?"

"That I'd have to check my schedule to see when I can fit them in. He also said something about wanting to come into the office and see you at work."

I run my hand through my dark hair as I lean my back against the built-in drawers. "He wants to come to the office?"

He leans his shoulder against the doorway, crossing his arms over his broad chest as he nods.

"What if they come in and someone tells them about us? Or what if he insists on seeing where I'm living?" My body fills with anxiety.

Theo sees this, and he walks over to me. He puts his hands on my biceps, gently rubbing them up and down. "Maybe it's time we come clean."

"What?" My voice is an octave too high.

He pulls me against his warm chest, and I wrap my arms around him. I let his heat sink into me as I breathe in the smell of his intoxicating cologne.

"I know you don't want to do that, but I think it would be better received coming from us than him just figuring it out himself." He kisses the top of my head as he combs his fingers through my hair.

Having him hold me does exactly what I needed it to do: distract me from the stresses of the outside world. The moment Theo and I met, I felt the undeniable attraction, and the moment we touched, everything else fell away. He and I have always created our own little world, and that holds true to this day. Feeling him against me makes my blood warm, and that throbbing starts between my thighs.

I kiss his chest, and his back straightens. I lift myself onto my tiptoes and kiss his collarbone and then his neck. His hand fists my hair, and he pulls my mouth to his, kissing me slow but hard and deep. I wrap my arms around his neck, pulling him closer, and he picks me up against him before moving across the small room and pressing my back to the wall.

Now that he has me pinned, his hands are free to roam and explore, and they sure do. He touches all his favorite parts, all the parts that have me breathless with need for him. He fists my panties, and he rips them from my body. I gasp, but he silences it with another hard kiss. Dropping my panties to the floor, his hand moves between my legs, drawing my arousal from my body as he spreads it between my folds.

"Always so wet for me," he mutters against my lips, slides two fingers deep inside me, making me gasp in relief.

"Theo," his name comes out in a whimper.

He knows I'm too impatient for this, so when he hears the pleading in my tone, he pushes his pants and boxers down until his long, hard cock springs free. Taking himself in hand, he positions himself at my entrance, and then he shoves forward, sliding into me with a growl. The connection makes us both call out.

"Oh, fuck Kay," he breathes, thrusting deeper.

I dig my nails into his back, and his back arches to get away from the pain, but a little bit of pain is exactly what he needs because it makes him fuck me harder, faster until we're both screaming with our release.

* * *

His brows lift, and he smiles at me from across the table in the busy restaurant. "Worked up an appetite, huh?" He takes a bite of his cheesy garlic bread.

I chuckle and wipe my mouth with my napkin. "What can I say? You can do that to a girl."

He grins and winks, making my heart race.

After having to hide our relationship for an entire year, I love getting to go out with him like this, but I hate that we're always seated with a table between us. I want to be able to reach out and touch him whenever I want. I want to hold hands. I want to rest my head on his shoulder. I want to kiss him where everyone can see. Theo Miller is mine, and I no longer have to hide that fact.

"Come sit on this side of the booth."

He looks at me with confusion written on his face. "What?"

"I don't like you being so far away. I want you next to me."

He smirks. "You want us to both sit on the same side of the booth?"

I nod. "For an entire year, we couldn't be seen in public together. Now, we can, and I want everyone to know you're mine. I want to touch you, kiss you whenever I want, and I can't do that with you all the way over there."

The fire I often see in his eyes is back. "Well, when you put it like that ..." He stands and moves to my side.

I scoot so he can sit on the outside. "That's better." My hand moves to his jaw, and I direct his mouth to mine. Our kiss isn't gross or showy, but it's long and slow. I don't care if we draw attention to ourselves. In fact, that's exactly what I want. I want everyone to know we're together, that he's mine, and I'm his.

After a moment, I pull back and break our kiss. His eyes open and lock with mine, slightly hooded. "I love you, gorgeous," he whispers, his hand cupping my jaw, his lips nearly touching mine.

"I love you too," I reply, kissing him once more. As I'm trying to pull away, he nips my bottom lip, making me giggle. I jerk and smack his arm, and he chuckles.

"What the hell is going on here?"

It feels like the air has been sucked from the room. I try to suck in a breath, but my lungs are frozen from hearing that voice. Theo and I both feel the coldness radiating toward our table, and we look up, now face-to-face with my dad and stepmom.

They're looking at us with confusion, anger, and disgust. And I'm looking up at them, probably resembling a deer in the headlights. I'm not afraid to tell them. I'm not even worried about how they'll take the news. I'm a grown woman, and I don't have to explain myself, but I am worried about how my dad will react toward Theo. I can only pray that being in public will help to keep his temper in check.

I squeeze Theo's bicep, and it gets his attention. He looks from my dad to me. He takes a deep breath, sending me a message with his eyes that I nod in agreement to.

He looks back to my father. "Asher, Meredith, would you like to join us?"

THEO

Asher shakes his head, his green eyes moving back and forth between me and his daughter. "I don't understand what's going on." He's holding his hands up like he's waiting to receive a passed tray.

Meredith takes a deep breath, and she smooths over her shocked expression. "Something tells me that if we sit down, things will be explained, Ash." She touches his bicep, trying to urge him into the booth, but he doesn't budge.

"I don't want to sit. I want to know why my friend and my daughter are sitting in this restaurant together, doing inappropriate things." His angry eyes focus on mine. "Explain. Now."

I nod, trying to keep my tone even. I don't want him to think that I'm angry because I'm not, but I also don't want him to think that he's threatening me in some way because I won't stand for it. I once again gesture toward the seat. "Please. Everything will be explained. I promise." I keep my voice quiet. "Look around you, Asher. We're in public. Let's not make a scene. Let's talk like adults."

He jerks his eyes from mine, and they quickly sweep the restaurant. He takes a deep breath and nods. Meredith takes a relieved breath, and she slides into the booth. Asher does the same, sitting across from me.

"Now, explain," he demands in a quiet but threatening tone.

I look at Kay, and she looks at me.

Wetting her lips, she says, "You remember the night when I was supposed to come over for dinner to meet Theo?"

Ash nods. "Of course. You didn't make it because you said you had a lot to do to prepare for the start of the school year."

She nods. "That is what I said, but it was a lie. The truth is, my friends were going out, and I hadn't gotten to party with them all summer because I stayed with mom. I had that breakup, and I just wanted to avoid him and his friends. But when I came home, the girls talked me into going out with them."

He doesn't look happy to learn that his daughter would rather party with her friends than join him for dinner, but he doesn't say anything.

"Anyway, I went out to the club that night. Me and the girls, we had drinks. We laughed and talked, danced, and flirted with guys to get them to buy our drinks." She looks at her stepmom. "You know, typical girls' night stuff."

Meredith nods.

"Well, one of the guys I met that night was Theo."

Both of them look from Kay to me, but Kay speaks again, drawing their attention away.

"We had both been drinking, and we had no idea of this connection we shared because we hadn't met yet." She shrugs. "We had a couple of drinks, talked, and hit it off." She swallows, and her eyes fall to the table between us. "I went home with him that night."

Asher's eyes fall closed, and his hand that's on the table tightens into a fist.

"Dad, I know you like to pretend that I'm some perfect little angel, but the truth is that I was a senior in college who had just gotten out of a long relationship. I was looking for a little fun before the school year started. Going to a club, drinking, and hooking up with a guy you just met is completely normal for a woman my age."

Meredith covers Asher's hand with hers. "He knows this, Kaylee. He remembers being a senior in college himself."

"Anyway, neither of us knew what we'd done until Monday morning, when we ended up in class together. We didn't know how to handle it or how to act. So we both just kind of avoided one another for a while, but the whole time, I couldn't stop thinking about the man who I met and how I felt something with him that I'd never felt with anyone else."

"And I felt the same way, Asher," I add on. "This isn't about getting with a younger woman. Kay and I share a connection, a connection we both recognized the night we met. And it was that connection that kept pulling us together, even when we both tried to forget."

"Eighteen years. There's an eighteen year difference between you two," he reminds us.

"It doesn't feel like it, though," Kay tells him.

Asher frowns at her.

"There's like a ten year difference between you and Meredith. Does it feel like it to you?" she asks.

He and Meredith look at one another.

"She has a point, Asher," Meredith tells him.

Asher shakes his head, and he pinches the bridge of his nose. Then acknowledgment hits him, and he looks up at us. "So, this started when you were still employed by the university?"

Neither of us answer, unsure if this is some kind of trap.

Meredith takes Asher's hand in hers. "Look at me."

He waits a moment, but then gives in, moving his eyes to hers.

"I don't know what you think you're about to do, but I suggest you drop it. Your daughter already told you how this happened. And I know you don't like it, but you're not going to try and trap them into something to get Theo in trouble. He's no longer employed by the university. Kaylee no longer attends the university. And neither of them are going to admit to breaking any rules. It's too late anyway. What you need to do is accept the fact that your little girl has grown up. She's a woman who is supporting herself, and it's her right to make her own choices. You don't have to like it, but you do need to respect it."

Kay leans in. "Thank you, Meredith," she whispers.

Asher takes a long breath, and he leans back in the booth, running his hand over his face. "So, there's nothing I can do here. Neither of you care that I don't like this? It doesn't bother you that by doing this, you're hurting your father?" he asks, looking at Kay. Then his eyes turn to me. "You don't care that you're seeing a woman against her father's wishes? You don't care that this will damage our friendship beyond repair?"

I take Kay's hand in mine. "If the roles were reversed, would you care? Would you give up your wife because someone else didn't like it?"

"You're not married."

"Yet," I add on. "This isn't just some fling, Asher. Kaylee and I have been together for over a year. We lived in secret for a year just to hold onto what we found. Then we moved back to New York together, and she's lived here, in my apartment, for three months. I love your daughter, and she loves me, and I will make her my wife one day. When she's ready."

He shakes his head. "And what about kids? Have you thought of that? You've never wanted kids, and now you're too old to even think about having them. Is my daughter going to have to miss out on motherhood to be with you?"

"If she wants kids, I'll give her kids. She's not going to miss out on anything because of me."

"Dad, Theo and I have already talked about this. We don't want kids," she tells him.

He looks at her. "Is that his decision or yours?"

She shakes her head. "I don't want kids. I never have."

This seems to take him by surprise. "You're young, Kaylee. You may change your mind one of these days."

"I won't," she tells him. "I decided a long time ago that I didn't want kids. After growing up with a split family … I never wanted to do that to another person. Having kids means you need to be selfless. You give up parts of your life to better theirs. Or, at least, you should."

We know it's a jab at him and the way he wasn't around when she was little.

Asher's eyes soften. "Kaylee, don't let my mistakes play a role in the decisions you make for yourself."

"You weren't selfless enough to have a kid. All you cared about was getting your degree, getting a job. And then you ended up cheating on Mom and leaving us. I watched her struggle every single day to work and provide for me. We're different in many ways, Dad, but one way we're the same is that I'm not selfless enough to have children either. The difference is that I'm smart enough to know that. I don't want to give up a part of my life to raise a child. I want to focus on my career. I want to come home from a busy day at work and be able to relax with the man I love. Every spare second I have, I want to give it to him or use it for myself. I want to be able to pack up and travel the world at the drop of a hat. I want to enjoy life and live. I want my life to be mine."

Asher stands and motions for Meredith to stand with him, then he looks down at us. "I can see that there is nothing I can do here. You're an adult, Kaylee. I can't run your life for you, and I can't change your mind. Just know that I do not like this. I do not approve." Then he looks at me. His eyes narrow. "Consider our friendship over, Theo. From this moment forward, I will treat you like the man my daughter is seeing. If you don't take care of her, you'll have me to deal with."

I don't like it, but it's to be expected. His world took a big shift today. It's only fair for him to be upset and bothered by the way things turned out. I can respect his decision, but I hope time heals these wounds for him. I hope that one day, he can consider me a friend again. "I understand." I hold out my hand to shake.

His chest expands with his deep breath, but he slaps his hand in mine and shakes it with no emotion on his face. I nod a thank you, and release his hand. He turns and walks away, with his wife following along behind him.

I look at Kay, and she lifts her brows and lets them fall. "At least that's over with."

I chuckle and squeeze her hand. "Let's get out of here. Suddenly, I'm not so hungry." I drop some cash on the table to cover our bill, and then the two of us head home.

We don't say much on the drive home, as we both have a lot to think about. It isn't until we're both in the clawfoot bathtub that she speaks on dinner.

She's sitting in front of me in the tub with her back against my chest. Her head is leaned back against my shoulder, and my arms are wrapped around her.

"Did you mean what you said at dinner?"

"I meant everything I said about dinner, but I don't know which part you're referring to."

She sits up and spins around to face me. "The part where you said that you would make me your wife one of these days."

"Of course I meant that. You really think I could live the rest of my life without being able to call you my wife?"

She grins. "I want that too. I want to elope, and I don't want to tell anyone. I don't want to invite anyone. I just want it to be us, the way it's been from the beginning."

Hearing her words only makes me think of the dream I had long ago, where we got married on my yacht in the middle of the ocean. "Just us," I agree.

She starts climbing into my lap, straddling me. "Nothing big or fancy. Just you and me, two rings, and preferably someplace warm." She laces her fingers into the back of my hair.

"I once dreamed that we got married on my yacht in nothing but our bathing suits."

She smiles. "I like that idea."

"Yeah?"

She nods. "Yes." She leans in, kissing me. "Ask me," she whispers against my lips.

I pull back, looking into her eyes. "Now?"

She nods.

"I don't have a ring."

She frowns. "I don't care about a ring, Theo."

My hands move to her hips, holding her in place on my lap. "The night we met is a night I'll never forget. That night changed the course of my life. I looked down, and our eyes locked. My heart raced, and my whole body grew warm and tingly. I knew then that you were going to mean something to me; I just didn't know what. Then we kissed, and I knew exactly what it was. I knew you were my other half. I knew I could run and hide, but I'd never be able to resist you for long. When we come together, it's more than just our bodies. It's our souls. When they connect, they create this beautiful, blinding light that I can't see past. That light is what warms me from the inside. It's the center of this world we're creating. I know I'll never be able to go back to living without you, Kay. I don't know what life has in store for us, but I know it's better than anything I could imagine because I'll have you at my side. I'm sorry I'm not prepared with a ring, but if you agree to marry me, I swear I'll get one tomorrow. I'll carry you out to the middle of the ocean, and I'll make you mine. I won't rest until we share a last name, until we're connected in every possible way two people can connect. Will you marry me, beautiful?"

She smiles as she blinks back tears. "Yes." Her arms tighten around my neck, and she pulls my mouth to hers, kissing me breathless. My heart is racing, pounding against my chest with excitement. The harder my heart beats, the more alive my body becomes. Suddenly, it doesn't matter that we were together just a few hours ago. The only thing I can think about is sliding inside her so I can be warmed by the light our connecting souls create.

Tightening my hold on her, I stand up from the tub with her in my arms, and I carry her to our bed. It doesn't matter that we're making a mess or that we're soaking the bed. All that matters is that we're in love, we're going to get married, and we no longer have to hide.

"Theo?"

I pull my lips from her neck, leaning back to look into her eyes.

"I love you." And those words are shining in her intense green eyes.

I thrust forward, sliding into her. I'm instantly blinded by the light of our love. "I love you too."

THE END

Share the Love!

If Kaylee and Theo's story captivated you, take a moment to share the love with the wider world.

Simply by sharing your honest opinion of this book and how you enjoyed it, you'll help new readers find their next great romance. Be careful not to give away any spoilers, though!

Thank you so much for your support. Every writer writes for their readers; thank you for helping me to find mine.

Scan the QR code below

REFERENCES

Allmer, Chris. "Forbidden Love Quotes." Blinkist Magazine. Last modified June 19, 2023. https://www.blinkist.com/magazine/posts/forbidden-love-quotes

www.ingramcontent.com/pod-product-compliance
Lightning Source LLC
Chambersburg PA
CBHW030609310726
48979CB00003B/633

* 9 7 9 8 9 9 0 9 3 1 1 1 4 *